# BLOOD RAGE

Jackson stopped when he saw Raider waiting for him with another pick handle raised high. The two men began to circle one another cautiously, the pick handles held out in front of them as each looked for an opening.

They suddenly seemed to come together, almost as if by prearrangement, pick handles swinging hard, each man intent on ending it now. The pick handles glinted in the sun as they were swung repeatedly. Panting, bloodied, hurting, they continued to go after one another, evenly matched, until Raider remembered what Jackson had said in the cantina, his comments about what he and the others had done to Sarah, how much he had enjoyed it, and now a mad killing rage swept over Raider, a red mist of fury, and he charged in, oblivious to pain, to danger, wanting only to kill.

First he broke Jackson's left arm . . .

The *Raider* Series *by*
*J. D. HARDIN*

# RAIDER

## VENGEANCE RIDE

J.D. HARDIN

**B**

BERKLEY BOOKS, NEW YORK

VENGEANCE RIDE

A Berkley Book/published by arrangement with
the author

**PRINTING HISTORY**
Berkley edition/January 1988

ISBN: 0-425-10556-3

A BERKLEY BOOK ® TM 757,375
Berkley Books are published by the Berkley Publishing Group,
200 Madison Avenue, New York, NY 10016
The name "BERKLEY" and the "B" logo
are trademarks belonging to the Berkley Publishing Corporation.

PRINTED IN THE UNITED STATES OF AMERICA

10  9  8  7  6  5  4  3  2  1

# CHAPTER ONE

He rode into town at dusk, materializing out of the growing darkness with disturbing suddenness. He did not come straight on in, but halted just beyond the first buildings, where he sat his mount motionlessly, studying the street ahead of him. Perhaps two minutes passed before, apparently satisfied, he urged his mount into a slow walk down the town's main street.

He was a big man, riding a big roan stallion. He was wearing a battered black Stetson, a short leather horseman's jacket, denim trousers, and well-worn handmade riding boots. At first glance he might have been taken for a cowboy coming in off the range, but there were elements in his appearance that suggested otherwise. For instance, his clothes, while showing trail wear, were cleaner than the average cowboy's, and his neckerchief was small and made of silk, very unlike the average trail hand's huge cotton bandanna, designed for wiping trail dust from one's face while following a herd, or for tying one's hat on in a strong wind.

Nor was the holster riding his right hip the usual worn,

soft chunk of leather used by most cowboys, who were more interested in protecting their pistols than in getting to them quickly. The top of this particular holster had been cut away, baring the rider's big Remington revolver halfway down the cylinder, with most of the trigger guard accessible. A heavy-caliber rifle with an unusually long barrel was housed in a saddle scabbard under the rider's left leg, the butt jutting upward within easy reach.

But it was his eyes that most gave the rider away. They were hard and black, glittering coldly above a heavy black mustache that curled down the sides of his mouth. No, he might be a man of the trail, but the newcomer did not appear to be the type of man who worked for a daily wage.

He continued down the street, facing forward, but his eyes were constantly in motion, missing nothing on either side. It was a very small town, just the one main dusty street, with three other short streets, more like alleys, cutting across it. There were no more than a couple of dozen buildings in the entire town, most of them made of weathered, warped pine planking. A rickety boardwalk ran partway down either side of the main street, for when rain turned the street into a muddy morass. In some sections of the boardwalk, planks had caved in, waiting for the careless foot. None of this mattered to the horseman. It was people he was watching for. Other men, armed like himself.

There was a saloon halfway down the main street. It was overlarge for such a small town, but seemed to fit in nevertheless. The horseman stopped the big roan in front of the saloon, seemed to deliberate a moment, then quickly dismounted, but with the reins still firmly in his hand. He stood behind his horse for a few seconds, out of the light that spilled weakly from between the saloon's low swinging doors. Seemingly satisfied again, the stranger took his horse over to the hitching rack and secured it by tying the reins to the wooden bar in such a way that one sharp tug on the end of the reins would instantly free them.

His hand strayed to the butt of the big rifle, pulling the barrel partway out of its scabbard. Then he seemed to think better of what he was doing and pushed the rifle firmly back into place. Walking around his horse, he stepped up onto the boardwalk, heading toward the saloon; but when he reached the entrance he moved to one side and glanced over the top of the swinging doors, with most of his body protected by the outside wall.

A quick glance inside seemed to reassure him. He stepped in through the doorway, quickly moving to his right, close against the wall, while his eyes did another quick reconnaissance of the saloon's interior. There was one man at the bar, apparently a cowhand. Further back, a small knot of men were seated around a table near the rear wall. The stranger's eyes flicked off the cowhand and settled on the men at the table. One of them looked up and met his eyes. Breaking his gaze away, the newcomer walked over to the bar, heading for the angle where it arced toward the side wall, so that he could stand facing the entire room, the door, and particularly the men seated at the rear table. "Bartender," he called out in a low but carrying voice.

The bartender had been half dozing at the far end of the bar. He jerked fully awake now, glared accusingly at the lone cowboy, then finally noticed the newcomer in his corner. Years of dealing with thirsty men warned him that this was not a man to disappoint, so he hurried down the bar. "What'll it be, stranger?"

"A beer. Then whiskey."

While the bartender went to fetch the drinks, the stranger seemed to relax a little. The bartender returned with a big mug of beer with foam trailing down one side, a half-full bottle of whiskey, and a chipped but usable glass. While the bartender was pouring whiskey into the glass the stranger drained the beer in several huge swallows. He sighed with pleasure, then placed his hand on the bartender's arm when he started to turn away. "Leave the bottle."

"Uh, yeah . . . sure."

The stranger took more time with the whiskey, sipping it slowly, standing half slouched against the bar, but always with his feet planted beneath him, ready to explode into action if the situation suddenly required it. While not appearing to do so, he was observing the room as intently as when he had first entered, so he noticed one of the men at the rear table nod to another man sitting next to him, then nudge him. The second man grinned, nodded back, then slowly got up from his chair and started walking slowly across the barroom. To the man at the bar there was no question of where the other man was heading, or what was going to happen, but he gave no notice of what he was thinking, rather seemed to relax even more, one elbow on the scarred and pitted bar top, his glass of whiskey held lightly in his right hand.

The other man walked to the swinging doors, leaned meaty forearms on them until they creaked from the weight, then looked out into the dusk, straight at the stranger's tethered horse. "Sorry-lookin' bag o' bones," he said loudly. "Real buzzard-bait."

One of the men at the rear table laughed. Not the one who'd nudged the man now at the door, but another one, a fat, dirty man with a drinker's huge red-veined nose. The stranger made no response, simply continued sipping his whiskey, seemingly looking off into space at nothing.

"That your nag?" the man at the door asked, turning toward the bar.

The stranger remained looking straight ahead. He took another sip of whiskey, shifted his weight a little as if looking for a more comfortable position.

"Hey!" the man by the door said sharply. "I was askin' you a question."

"Thataway, Moose," the fat man at the rear table said loudly, grinning.

Now the man at the bar turned to face the man by the door. Moose. The name fit. He was big, meaty, with a massive head and thick body. His nose was broken, his ears smashed. His eyes were small and piggish, crowded in close toward that mashed nose.

"I asked if that was your horse," Moose repeated.

The stranger slowly looked Moose up and down. He

took a sip of whiskey, then spat out a little. The way he did it was subtly insulting. "Where I come from," he finally said, "it's kinda unhealthy to take a whole lotta interest in another man's horse."

Moose blinked, surprised. He was accustomed to other men's fear, and this stranger was not showing any fear at all. For a moment his face showed indecision. Perhaps he was thinking that it might be a good idea to back off, but he glanced over at the table where he had been sitting, and the looks of anticipation on the faces of the men there told him that he could not back down. Not without being made to look bad.

"What's your name?" Moose demanded.

"Where I come from, that's not too smart a question either," the stranger replied.

"Look, asshole . . ."

"My name sure as hell isn't asshole."

"Maybe not, but it's gonna be mud 'fore I get through with you," Moose snarled, stepping quickly toward the stranger. Later, nobody was able to sort out exactly what happened, because it happened so quickly. One moment the stranger was slouched against the bar, sipping his whiskey, with Moose bearing down on him, and the next moment Moose was on the floor. The bartender, who was closest, claimed that the stranger first threw the contents of his whiskey glass into Moose's face, and while Moose was pawing at his eyes, simply hooked a boot toe behind Moose's rear heel, smashed his open palm straight into his face, and sent him down onto his back.

By the time Moose stopped bouncing, the stranger was back at the bar, pouring himself another shot of whiskey, concentrating on his task as if Moose were not lying on the floor only a couple of yards away. When his glass was full, the stranger leaned against the bar once again and resumed sipping his whiskey.

Moose rolled ponderously to his feet, roaring with rage. "You sonova—" he started to shout, rushing forward. The stranger set his glass down and stepped to the right, hooking his left fist into Moose's gut. Moose grunted, and bent forward slightly, not really hurt—until the stranger grabbed him by the hair and yanked his head downward, hard.

Moose's mouth smashed against the edge of the bar. Everyone in the room heard the meaty thump of it, mixed with the sharper crack of breaking teeth. The stranger then repeated his earlier move, hooking his foot behind Moose's heel and sending him down onto his back. Then he once again picked up his drink and resumed sipping it as if nothing unusual had happened.

Moose remained on the floor a little longer this time, his arms splayed out to the sides. Then he sat up, shaking his head and spitting out pieces of broken teeth. He wiped his hand across his mouth. It came away wet with his own blood. He stared at the back of his hand for a moment, then, screaming with rage, he lurched to his feet and charged the stranger once again.

The stranger sighed, put down his drink, stepped out of the way of Moose's lumbering charge, clubbed him in the back of the neck as he went by, driving Moose into the rear wall next to the bar, spun him around, hit him in the jaw with his left fist, temporarily stunning him, then shifted his weight forward, pushing his left palm up against Moose's nose, forcing his head back, which released the tension in Moose's stomach muscles. The stranger then hit him hard, very hard, sinking his fist deep into Moose's diaphragm. Air exploded from Moose's ruined mouth, spraying more blood and teeth, and he doubled over forward, his breath wheezing hoarsely as he fought for air.

For the next couple of minutes Moose staggered in circles, his hands pressed to his midsection, trying to get his breathing under control. Meanwhile, the stranger was back at the bar, once again paying attention to his drink, slouching unconcernedly.

That was what finally pushed Moose over the edge—the way the stranger kept returning to his drink each time he beat the shit out of him. While Moose was fighting to get his wind back, the stranger could have done anything he wanted to him. He could have beaten him half to death, he could have kicked him, he could have broken bones. Instead, he had treated him as if he were an annoying yapping mongrel that a few well-aimed stones would drive away.

That kind of contempt Moose could not take. He was aware of the snickers coming from the table he had so recently vacated. Many of the men there had no love for him; he had a habit of using his great strength to humiliate smaller men. "You son of a bitch," he snarled, once he could breathe again. He was wearing a pistol on his right hip, and now he went into a crouch as he reached for it. His sole aim in life now was to destroy the man leaning against the bar sipping whiskey, the man who had beaten him.

If the onlookers had so far been impressed by the way the stranger handled himself, it was now time for them to be genuinely amazed, because the stranger suddenly exploded into the fastest action any of them had ever seen. One moment he was lounging against the bar, the whiskey glass in his right hand, the next moment that hand was filled with his big Remington .44. Everyone flinched, waiting for the blast of gunfire. Moose's pistol was still coming up, although the stranger had clearly already beaten him, but instead of shooting, the stranger simply rapped the barrel of his pistol against the back of Moose's wrist. Hard. Very hard. Moose howled in pain, dropping his pistol.

The stranger, showing his first indication of anger so far, stepped forward, smashing his gun barrel twice across Moose's face, first the right side, then the left. Moose staggered backward, blood pouring from deep cuts. He would have fallen, but the stranger caught him by the front of his shirt, spun him around, then kicked him straight out the swinging doors, planting his boot deep into Moose's broad buttocks. Moose caught at the swinging doors as he went though, tearing one loose and taking it with him, then he disappeared into the night. Everyone in the room could hear the crash and thud when he hit the boardwalk, then rolled into the street.

The stranger immediately turned back to face the room, his .44 still in his hand. No one moved. The bartender stood frozen, one hand low under the bar. Smiling nervously, he slowly raised his hand, showing the bar rag he was holding.

The men at the table where Moose had been sitting were sitting very still, all hands in plain view on the table. The stranger remained facing them for a moment, tense, ready to move. Then, when it appeared that they were going to remain motionless, he finally holstered his pistol, turned back to the bar, and once again picked up his drink.

The bar remained quiet for another few minutes, except for a rising buzz of conversation at the rear table. Finally, one of the men got up and began walking toward the stranger. It was the man who had first said something to Moose, the man who had nudged him in the stranger's direction.

He was a big man, too, but of a totally different caliber than Moose, more muscle than fat. He walked with sureness and balance. Each movement he made hinted at speed. His face showed a certain animal brutality, but there was something more there, too, a cold, calculating menace that had been missing underneath Moose's angry bluster. Suddenly the stranger was no longer leaning against the bar but was standing square on his feet, whiskey glass back on the bar, both hands free.

The big man came up to him. They were both big men, the stranger perhaps a little taller, the other man thicker through the body. "Relax," the other man said. "Moose is an asshole. He got what he deserved."

"I kinda thought you mighta sicced him onto me," the stranger said quietly.

The other man shrugged. "Yeah . . . maybe. Maybe I just wanted to see what you were made of."

"Well, did you see?"

"Oh, yeah, sure. You can handle yourself, all right. I like that. I like a man who can take care of himself. Here . . . lemme buy you a drink."

The stranger continued looking coldly at the other man. "Aw, come on. No hard feelin's," the other said. "We get kinda bored around here. Gawd, this is one shit-eatin' little hole of a town. You livened up our day. Come on, take the drink."

The man was signaling to the bartender, who came sprinting over with another glass, then began filling both the stranger's glass and the other man's. The stranger finally nodded and reached out for the glass. The other man smiled, picked up his own glass, raised it. "Name's Jackson," he said. "People around here call me Breaker."

The stranger raised his own glass. "Raider," he said. "Just Raider."

"Yeah? Strange name."

"So's Breaker."

Jackson unconsciously flexed his massive shoulders. "Not really," he replied.

There was a sudden loud clumping of boots on the boardwalk outside, then the remaining swinging door was thrust violently aside and Moose appeared in the doorway, blood running down his face, his eyes wild with rage and pain—and with an enormous shotgun held in both hands. "You bastard!" Moose screamed. "I'm gonna blow you all the way to hell!"

It was the very length of the shotgun barrel that saved Raider; it took time to swing it, and by the time it tracked onto where Raider had been standing a moment before, he was no longer there. Raider spun to the right, Jackson to the left. The roar of the big shotgun was deafening inside the saloon, the concussion so intense that the windows bulged outward under the pressure, but the massive load of shot missed Raider by more than a foot, shattering an entire row of bottles behind the bar. Moose tried to turn, to bring the other barrel to bear on Raider, but it was too late. Raider's pistol was already in his hand, the hammer snicking back into full cock, and an instant later 240 grains of lead plowed into Moose's chest.

Moose staggered backward, the shotgun discharging again, this time blowing a hole in the ceiling. Raider fired a second time, the bullet taking Moose in the throat. Moose spun around, collided with the wall, desperately

clawed at its rough pine surface, then slowly slid downward, leaving a broad smear of blood behind him on the
wood. He was dead by the time he finally hit the floor.

Once again the stranger spun around to face the room. It
was a moment before he finally relaxed. Jackson was
standing a little to one side, with both his hands plainly
visible, far from the butt of his revolver. The remaining
men at the rear table had scattered for cover after the first
blast of Moose's shotgun, and were clearly not in a mood
for any further trouble. Raider slowly shucked the two
empties out of his pistol, replacing them with fresh rounds,
then slipped the big Remington back into its holster.

Jackson's lips twitched into a small grin. "Guess maybe
you're even better with a pistol than you are with your
hands."

"Good enough."

A small nod from Jackson. "It makes a man wonder just
how good."

"You in a mood to find out?"

Jackson laughed. "Nope. That's enough fun and games
for tonight."

He turned back to the bar. Both his and Raider's glasses
were where they had left them. He picked up his and
handed the other to Raider. "Up yours," he said, still grinning. Raider, with no expression showing on his face,
raised his glass and drank. Then he put his glass back
down on the bar and pointed to Moose's body. 'What kinda
trouble is there gonna be about him?"

Jackson shrugged. "Well, there ain't no real law around
these parts, an' he did come in here blastin' away with a
scattergun. But I'll tell you—it's kinda our custom around
these parts that you put up some scratch to help plant whoever you shoot. You know—for the undertaker. The bar-
keep'll be happy to take the money."

Raider fished in his pocket and came up with a ten-
dollar gold piece, which he rang down onto the bar top.
"He ain't' worth it," he muttered, jerking his chin toward
what was left of Moose. "Now, maybe I'd like to hang
around and jaw a little, but I'm tired as hell. Been in the

saddle one hell of a long time. Is there any decent place to stay around here?"

"Well, I don't know if you'd call it decent, but there's a hotel down the street. Pritchard's place. Ain't got more'n its share o' bedbugs an' fleas. Cheap, too."

"That's where I'm heading, then," Raider said, turning and moving toward the door. He glanced back at the bartender. "Take my drinks outta that ten bucks. Then use the rest to plant that tub o' lard deep enough so that he don't stink up the town."

He left then, moving out the door smoothly, never really turning his back on the room. Breaker Jackson remained at the bar, nursing his whiskey until another man got up from the rear table and came over to him. He was considerably smaller than Jackson, but he moved with a pantherish grace that developed immediate respect in any man who met him. "Some hombre," the smaller man said. "A real catamount."

"Yeah. Handles himself real well. Course it was only Moose. Too bad about ol' Moose. Hmmmnnn...Raider, he said his name was. Might be kinda interestin' to go toe to toe against him."

The smaller man laughed. "An' it might hurt a little, too. One thing I noticed about him—there's a man on the run if I ever saw one."

Jackson nodded. "Yeah, Ernie, I think you might be right. Yeah, that's real interestin'. You know, this Raider hombre might work out all right for us."

# CHAPTER TWO

It was completely dark by the time Raider left the saloon. The hotel that Breaker Jackson had recommended was less than fifty yards away, but, being a horseman, and therefore constitutionally adverse to walking when he could ride, Raider pulled his horse's reins loose, swung up into the saddle, and rode the short distance to the hotel.

It was a rambling two-story structure, of the usual local pine-board construction, leaning a little to one side, probably pushed in that direction by the prevailing wind. Raider rehitched his horse in front of the hotel, which bore no other sign out front other than a warped pine board on which was written in faded letters, "Pritchard House." His boots thudded loudly on the boardwalk as he headed toward the hotel's front door. Entering, he found himself in a fairly good-sized if unappealing room, which might have passed for a lobby if there had been any furniture. A low counter was situated on the far side of the room, but there was no one behind it, only a rather large hand bell. Raider picked it up and rang it vigorously. Either the bell was made of some kind of pot metal or it was cracked, because it gave off only a tinny rattle.

Apparently that was enough. A few seconds later a door opened behind the counter and a man stepped into view. He was thin, somewhere between fifty and sixty years old, and looked as sour as a lemon. He grunted a sound somewhere between "Yump?" and "Yeah?" to which Raider replied, "Got any rooms?"

There was another indistinguishable reply, which probably meant yes because the man fished a key out from beneath the counter, dropped it on the wood, then added much more clearly, "Rooms'r thirty-five cents a day, wash water extra. No women in the rooms less'n you git 'em through me."

Raider nodded, although he considered thirty-five cents a day a bit high for this fleabag. However, it looked as if this were the only place in town, so he nodded and fished in his pocket for some coins, which he rang down onto the countertop. "Got a horse out front that'll take some lookin' after."

"Ten cents extra gits him a stall an' feed."

Another dime went down onto the countertop, at which the proprietor suddenly turned around and bellowed, "Jimmy!" while furiously ringing the dead-sounding bell.

In an amazingly short time a whip-thin boy of about thirteen or fourteen came sprinting out of a side door and skidded to a halt in front of the counter. "Yessir, Mr. Pritchard," he said, panting.

Pritchard sourly looked the boy up and down. "Took your own good goddamn time," he muttered. "This here gent's got a horse out front. Take the nag around to the stables an' see that it gets taken care of."

"I'll get my gear first," Raider said, turning to follow the boy, who was already sprinting toward the front door.

"Hell, let the boy git it. It'll give the lazy little bastard somethin' to do," Pritchard protested.

Raider turned and looked straight at Pritchard. "I said I'd get it," he replied flatly, at which Pritchard, after a good look into Raider's eyes, wisely shut his mouth.

By the time Raider got out onto the boardwalk, the boy, Jimmy, was already standing by his horse, stroking the animal's flanks. "Gee, nice horse, mister." But it was the big rifle the boy was mostly looking at.

Raider walked up to the boy, fished in his pocket, and flipped him a quarter. Jimmy was so surprised that he nearly let the coin fall into the dust, catching it only at the last minute. He opened his hand and stared at the quarter as if he'd never seen one before, which could easily have been the case—at least, seen one this close up, right in his own hand.

"The quarter's a little something extra, so's you'll rub the animal down," Raider said. "And give him plenty of feed. If I see he's bein' taken good care of, there'll be other quarters on down the line."

"Jesus . . . thanks, mister," Jimmy blurted out. "An' I'll put your saddle in the tack room."

"Uh-uh. Just lay it up next to the stall, in case I want to saddle up real quick."

Jimmy nodded, impressed. Raider began removing his traveling gear from his mount. There was very little of it, just a pair of saddlebags, a bedroll, and the rifle. The boy's interest remained high as Raider slid the big Winchester from its scabbard. "Holy God. Never seen a rifle like that before."

"Centennial Model," Raider replied. "Caliber .45-75. Big bullet, 350 grains. Shoots long and hits hard."

He had turned to go back into the hotel, saddlebags over his left shoulder, bedroll tucked under his left arm, rifle held in his right hand, when the boy asked in a choked and hesitant voice. "Uh . . . you the feller shot Moose?"

Raider turned toward Jimmy and gave him a long look that brought sweat to the boy's forehead. "I'll give you a little advice," he finally said. "If you want to live a long and healthy life, knock off askin' people questions like that."

Raider turned and pushed his way in through the hotel's front door, vanishing inside. Jimmy remained frozen in place for a few seconds, feeling the iciness of his sweat, then he quickly took the horse's reins and began leading it around toward the back of the hotel, where the stables were. "Holy shit," he kept muttering to himself, glancing from time to time at the quarter, which was still clenched tightly in his fist.

To Raider's surprise, the room he was shown into was not as bad as he'd expected, given the hotel's exterior and Pritchard's personality. True, it wasn't as clean as it might have been, and was rather lacking in furniture, but it was big, and the bed was good and hard, which meant that he wouldn't have to throw the mattress down onto the floor.

There was a jug of water waiting next to a not-too-badly-chipped washbasin. Raider poured some of the water into the basin, took off his shirt, and began to wash. He had a hard-muscled torso, the taut contours of which were broken here and there by old bullet and knife scars. After he had washed his face he began securing the room for the night. His first move was to wedge the back of a chair under the doorknob, then place a water glass on the chair seat, so that if anyone tried to slide the chair out of the way during the night, the glass would fall noisily to the floor.

His rifle he leaned against the wall near the head of the bed. His pistol went under the pillow. He then took off his boots and trousers and lay down on the bed with the single cover pulled only halfway up his body—it was a warm night. He spent a few minutes before going to sleep reviewing the day's events. Moose's death occupied him for a moment. He didn't much care for casual killing, but he suspected that if anyone deserved killing, it was probably Moose.

No point in bothering himself over what was past. All in all, it had been a productive day. He'd only been in town for an hour or so, and he'd already made contact with Breaker Jackson. Which, after all, was the reason he was here.

A few seconds later, Raider was asleep, a very light sleep, his senses alert for any sound. The glass remained on the chair seat. His right hand stayed half under the pillow near his pistol. His feet were constantly ready to hit the floor.

The next few days were days of relative inactivity for Raider. Most of his time was spent in the saloon where he had killed Moose. Fortunately, the man seemed to have had few friends; no one tried to avenge him. There was, in fact, a little good-natured joshing about the fight. It was that kind of town.

There were seldom many people in the saloon. The regular clientele centered around Breaker Jackson and his cronies. Jackson seemed to go out of his way to be friendly to Raider. Raider responded cautiously, but within a few days he was drinking regularly with Jackson. And with his sidekick, Ernie Duval. Raider had a little trouble warming to Duval. He was a small man, with quick graceful movements, which might have imparted a certain amount of appeal to his personality, had it not been for the crazed gleam in his dark, narrow eyes. Raider immediately pegged Duval as a man who killed because he loved killing. And, as Raider discovered, when Duval killed, he usually killed with a knife.

Duval was very good with a blade, in the sense that he could produce one and slip in into an opponent before the opponent was even aware that a knife was near. Duval always carried a knife secreted somewhere on his person, toward his back. It was hard to tell just where. Raider saw him use it in earnest one night. A stranger had come into the bar, a big man, well-hung with guns and obviously accustomed to using them. It did not take long to realize that the man was a natural bully, and since Ernie Duval was a rather small man, the stranger began to needle him, after downing a few glasses of the local rotgut whiskey.

For about half an hour, Ernie appeared to take the stranger's escalating insults quite meekly. Finally, his face twisted into a strange, lopsided smile and he walked up to the bigger man. "Ya know, stranger," he said in an amused voice, "you're the first man I ever met who shits through his mouth."

It took a second or two for the insult to sink into the stranger's whiskey-soaked brain, but eventually it did, and he stepped toward Ernie, snarling unintelligible insults. Ernie easily stepped away from the stranger's wild round-house swing, then kicked him neatly in the balls. The stranger grunted in shock, then bent forward, both hands pressed against his wounded crotch. Ernie simply stood there, smiling that weird smile, only a yard or two from the stranger, looking down at where his hands were. "How long you been playin' with yourself, you queer bastard?" he asked pleasantly.

The gunman, which was what the stranger was, immediately forgot the dull ache in his balls and straightened up, snarling a curse as his right hand streaked toward his holstered pistol. As fast as he was, Ernie was faster. He stepped forward smoothly, right inside the stranger's reach, placing his left hand on the other man's right wrist, so he couldn't complete his draw. Meanwhile, Ernie's right hand had disappeared behind him for a moment, and now it reappeared, moving with easy speed. There was a brief flash of steel, and then Ernie's right hand was pressed tightly against the stranger's midsection.

So far there was only a little blood to show where the knife had gone in, then the stranger's face went slack and sick with delayed shock. He grunted, his right hand dropping away from his gun butt as he attempted to push Ernie away. His grunt changed to a horrible scream as Ernie suddenly ripped the knife to one side, gutting him.

Ernie stepped back, withdrawing the knife. A huge gout of blackish blood jetted from a gaping wound in the stranger's midsection. He jackknifed forward, both hands clutching desperately at his belly, trying to hold in his guts, which were bulging out in grayish-green coils. He slowly looked up, his face a mask of agony. Ernie was still only a few feet away, grinning, holding the knife low in front of him.

The stranger tried to say something, failed, tried to move forward, stumbled, screamed, vomited. He should have fallen then, but, summoning up the will from somewhere within his gutted body, he jerked his right hand backward again, toward the butt of his pistol. He knew he was already a dead man, but he intended to take Ernie all the way to hell with him.

The smile never left Ernie's face. He stepped in again, this time driving the knife into the stranger's chest, right over the heart, then he stepped back to watch the final act.

The stranger's entire body had shuddered as the knife went into him for the second time. Strain distorted his facial muscles as he slowly pulled his pistol out of its holster. The pistol wavered. It was clear that he was not going to be able to bring it up to bear on Ernie. The muzzle jerked up another couple of inches but could go no further. A violent tremor shook the man's body, and he finally pitched forward onto his face. A few final leg twitches, and the man lay still.

No one else in the bar had said anything since the start of the fight. Now Breaker Jackson broke the silence. "Goddamn it, Ernie," he said good-naturedly. "You keep up this kinda thing, you're gonna make the undertaker one hell of a rich son of a bitch."

"Yeah," Ernie replied, giggling. "We're gonna have to do somethin' about his' rates."

"Uh-huh. We should get some kind of discount."

And it was left at that. There did indeed seem to be no law in the town, none that Raider could see, which at least had probably saved him from a lot of official hassling over Moose's killing. But Ernie Duval . . . he gave Raider the creeps. They all did, including Breaker Jackson. He'd like nothing better than to ride on out of here, maybe after having rid the world of the local human vermin. But he couldn't leave. Not yet. He had come here for a reason, and Breaker Jackson was part of that reason.

One night he discovered that matters were beginning to progress. He had left the saloon to return to his hotel room, and when he entered, he immediately saw that his room had been searched during his absence. There was nothing obvious about the search, but Raider had long ago devised subtle means of knowing when his belongings had been tampered with, means such as the precise and complicated placement of objects, or remembering where cobwebs had been. Now the signs said that he had had a visitor.

Raider carefully went through his bedroll, eventually withdrawing a crumpled piece of paper that had not been put back quite where he had left it. He held the paper up, glanced at the ornate printed heading. The words, "The Pinkerton National Detective Agency," arched across the top. Lower down there was a picture of a single unblinking eye, and beneath it, the logo, "We Never Sleep."

The reward was for five hundred dollars, the name and description Raider's. Wanted for robbery and murder. Raider smiled as he tucked the wanted poster back in place. Good. They'd bought it.

The next day he thought he saw a new look of interested speculation on Breaker Jackson's face. Raider passed that morning the same way he passed most mornings, sipping awful whiskey in the saloon. However, that afternoon he went into the stables at the back of Pritchard's hotel. Jimmy, who had been stretched out on a bale of hay, leaped to his feet, the fear draining from his face when he realized that it was not Mr. Pritchard, his employer, his tormentor who had come in, but instead Raider, his benefactor.

"Hey, Jimmy," Raider said. "Is that harness mender still hangin' around town?"

"Yeah, sure, Mr. Raider."

"Good. Give me my bridle. I want to get the side latches fancied up."

"Oh, hell, Mr. Raider. I'd be glad to take it on over for you."

Raider looked at the boy quizzically. Jimmy blushed. "It ain't that way, Mr. Raider. You wouldn't have to pay me nothin' at all."

Raider smiled. "I owe you another quarter anyhow, Jimmy, because of the way you been keepin' up my horse. Here."

He flipped the boy a quarter. Despite Jimmy's recent disavowal of monetary gain, his hand rose automatically and snatched the coin out of the air. He held it self-consciously. "I'll get that bridle right over to the—"

"Uh-uh. I want to do it myself, so's I can explain what it is I want him to do. Besides, it'll get me the hell outta that stinking saloon for a while."

Raider picked up the bridle and left the stable, half aware of the worshiping look that followed him. Damn it all, kid, he thought bitterly, go find yourself some decent heroes.

Raider found the harness mender sitting in front of a small lean-to on the edge of town. He was a traveling man, wandering around the countryside with one horse and a mule, mending harness at isolated ranches. About once a week he made it into town, apparently more to drink up his meager earnings in the saloon than for any business he might find here. The town was a bust as far as commerce was concerned. Whatever reason there might once have been for building a settlement here had long since vanished. The surrounding countryside was relatively barren, just a touch on the good side of being badlands. Rugged hills enclosed it on all sides. Perhaps the one feature that caused its continued existence was a reliable spring. That and its isolation from the law, which made it attractive to men like Breaker Jackson and Ernie Duval. And to Raider.

The harness mender was lounging against a log, sipping rotgut from a half-empty bottle. Raider tossed him the bridle. The harness mender listened silently as Raider detailed what work he wanted done. He was a medium-sized man, rawhide-hard after years of wandering a hard land. He always seemed to have the same two-week growth of beard, as if his facial hair never grew any longer. He was not a prepossessing man—if you didn't look into his eyes, which were a piercing gray in color. He usually kept his eyes cast down, but now he turned them full onto Raider. "McParland is wondering what's been goin' on with you. It's been ten days since you sent in your last report."

"Tell the bastard I ain't about to write nothin' down. They went through my stuff."

"Yeah? They find the wanted poster?"

"Uh-huh. A day or so ago."

"I bet they ate it right up. It was a first-class piece of work. As real-looking as they come."

"Yeah. Real enough to maybe encourage some yahoo to blow me apart for the five hundred dollars reward."

"Well, that's all part of this god-blessed, wonderful, fun-lovin' job, ain't it?"

"Guess so. Anyhow, what's the word? There been any more robberies?"

"Nope. But then, Jackson ain't left town even once, has he?"

"Nope. But we don't know for sure that he's in on it."

"He better be. It's the only lead we got."

"A mighty slim one. Jesus, what a son of a bitch he is. That nickname . . ."

"Breaker?" Yeah. Guess he earned it. The word is that he likes to beat men to death with his fists and his boots. Breaks 'em up into bloody chunks."

"Ernie Duval is with him."

"No shit!" the harness mender replied, whistling in surprise. "We didn't know that. Now, there's one weird little bastard."

"Uh-huh," Raider murmured, thinking about the man Duval had gutted. "I'd like to just go in there and sack all of their saddles and send 'em on up to Saint Pete for a little harp practice. You feel like helpin' me? We'd be doin' the world a real favor."

"Uh-uh. They gotta stay alive. Long enough to give us what we want."

"Easy for you to say. You don't have to hobnob with those shitheads every day."

The harness mender took a long critical look at his dusty, ragged clothing, at the calluses on his hands. "I ain't exactly livin' in clover. My momma never raised her little boy to be no wanderin' bum."

Raider grinned. "Lots of mothers gotta learn to live with disappointments."

"Like yours?" the harness mender grinned back.

"Yep. She never did quite figure out where she went wrong."

A moment's shared silent mirth, then the harness mender interjected, "What'll I tell McParland?"

Raider shrugged. "What *can* you tell him, except to keep his shirt on? If a break comes along, I kinda think it'll come real sudden. We're dealin' with a real cagey bunch. They don't much trust anybody. You just try and stay a little closer to town. Close as you can without makin' anybody think too much about you. I'll get you word."

"Yeah. Well, stay healthy. That can be a full-time job around these parts."

"You too. Just drop off the bridle with the kid that works in Pritchard's stable. That way, we won't be seen together too much."

A nod from the harness mender. Raider turned and walked away, toward town and the saloon, wishing he didn't have to be walking away from the only man in the area he could trust to back him up if the cards fell wrong.

# CHAPTER THREE

Raider was unprepared when Jackson finally came to him with the offer. He had not expected it so quickly, so all at once. He had imagined that there would be a lot of verbal feeling out first, lots of probing, then the actual proposition.

Raider had been spending another uneventful afternoon at the saloon, when Jackson walked up to him at the bar. "How'd you like to make a lot of money?" Jackson asked bluntly.

Raider shrugged. "Ain't got nothin' against it. Depends on what I gotta do to make it."

"Just what I expect you do best," Jackson replied, grinning.

"That don't include workin'."

"Hell, I know that. Course, it'll be a little dangerous. You know how it goes—the more danger, the more money."

"Yeah? Well, you ain't tellin' me much, are you? I'd like to hear the details."

"Uh-uh. No way. Either you're in or you're out, and

you come in blind. That's the way it's gotta be. But it's one hell of a lot of money. You could maybe pick up a thousand, even two thousand dollars for a couple of days' work."

Raider looked impressed. "That's good money. Tell you what. I'll think it over and—"

"Uh-uh. No thinkin'. It's now or not at all. If you decide yes, then we leave in an hour."

Raider remained silent for a few seconds. He suspected that if he said no, in another hour he'd probably be in big trouble. The offer had been made, it was out in the open. Not too much chance they'd let him live if he refused. "Okay, I'm in," he finally said. "I'll go on over and get my gear together."

Maybe he'd have a chance to leave a message with the stable boy, Jimmy, to be relayed to the harness mender. That plan was immediately shot down when Jackson said, "Good. I'll come along with you."

So they weren't going to let him out of their sight. A careful bunch. He made no complaint as Jackson walked with him to the hotel, where Raider asked Jimmy to ready his horse, then it was up to the room to gather his trail gear, with Breaker Jackson still at his side.

A short time later Ernie Duval rode up to the hotel stables, leading Jackson's horse, which was saddled, bridled, and outfitted for what looked like a long ride. The three of them rode out of town well before the expiration of the hour Jackson had earlier mentioned.

After they had ridden for a couple of hours, Raider finally asked, "Well, now that we're on our way, what can you tell me?"

Ernie Duval snickered. "We ain't gonna be working in no office, that's for sure."

"Shut up, Ernie," Breaker said quietly. Then he turned to Raider. "You know pretty much what it is we aim to do. The details can wait until we get where we're goin'. That's what it takes to keep outta trouble. Good planning."

Well, ol' hoss, Raider thought, I don't hardly think

you're the one who does that planning. You don't look like a man who could even plan a trip to the outhouse.

It was a long ride, more distance than they could cover in a single day, but by the time they made camp that night Raider had figured out that they were probably heading for Wyoming's Jackson Hole country. That made sense. The Jackson Hole badlands were a natural haven for outlaws and desperadoes of all kinds—way out on the left elbow of nowhere, and with terrain so rugged that it was hard to tell where you were. An intensely private place.

Raider could tell when they were nearing their destination. Late in the afternoon of the second day, Jackson and Duval, who had been riding pretty much without saying a word, began to become more animated "'Bout time we had us another payday," Duval said cheerfully. "That damned undertaker was eatin' up all my cash."

Jackson laughed. "We'll have to do him someday. See if we can get back our money."

"Then who'll bury the bastard. We need him, even if it's only to keep down the stink."

Cheered by this gentle trend in the conversation, Raider rode along morosely. He had been doing his best to keep track of where they were going, although he suspected that Jackson had led them into the badlands by a rather round-about route. The countryside was very rugged, a broken land, with numerous canyons winding between barren buttes, a land so little traveled that there were few established trails. A man would have to know just where he was going, and on top of that, have a lot of trail craft to get there.

For a while it looked as if Jackson might be lacking that trail craft. He and Duval began to argue about their direction. "I tell you, it lies over that way," Duval insisted.

"Ah, shit, Ernie, you can't even find your way outta the front door," Jackson grumbled. Nevertheless, he looked worried. He began to lead the three of them in wide sweeps, looking anxiously for landmarks. Raider had begun to think that maybe the whole thing might be called off because they were lost, when Duval finally let out a whoop and spurred his horse forward. "There it is, by God," he yelled.

A moment later he had disappeared. Raider kicked his horse into a canter, and then he saw it, a narrow cleft in the side of what had only a moment before looked like a solid wall of rock. Jackson pointed to the cleft, urging Raider to ride in through it. Raider hesitated a moment, hating to have the other man riding behind him in such tight quarters, but, realizing he had little choice, he rode on in.

The entranceway was very narrow, but almost immediately broadened out, and a moment later Raider rode out into a small natural amphitheater, an opening in the rock perhaps two hundred yards across, with solid walls of stone rising all around it. Raider doubted there was any way to get on top of those cliffs from the outside. This was as secure a hiding place as he had ever seen.

They were not the first ones to arrive. Several horses were wandering, unsaddled, near a pool of water that flowed from a small spring that gushed a clear stream from several yards up one of the rock walls. A man carrying a rifle suddenly popped up from behind a rock. His face cleared when he recognized Jackson and Duval, then tightened when he failed to recognize Raider. "Who the hell's that?" he demanded of Jackson.

"A new man. Don't you worry none about him."

The other man shrugged. "We'll see what the boss has to say about that."

Raider, Jackson, and Duval unsaddled their mounts, then set about cooking a meal. They had not bothered much about eating on the way, and all three of them were very hungry. While he ate, Raider studied the men around him. If he might have had any doubts before as to the nature of Jackson's offer, he had none now. This was as vicious-looking a crew as he'd ever seen. Highwaymen and killers, all of them.

Including himself, Jackson, and Duval, there were nine men. Quite a force, which fit in with the robberies that had been committed so far. It was always a substantial force, riding in fast, hitting hard, overpowering any resistance, then riding out as quickly as they had ridden in, laden with loot. Jackson had not been exaggerating. This was indeed a chance to make a lot of money—if a man got out of it alive.

Raider noticed that the men didn't seem to really know one another. They had all obviously been recruited by someone else. Smart. If one was caught, it wouldn't be easy to reach the others through him. Raider began to see the workings of a very intelligent mind behind all this, which did not surprise him, since the raids had so far been carried out with clockwork efficiency. And Jackson was obviously not the one who had done the planning, which was also not a surprise; since, while Breaker Jackson might exhibit a certain craftiness, he certainly could not be accused of being highly intelligent, and the leader of this group had been described by the few who had survived encounters with him as an urbane, clever, and cruel masked man.

It was nearly dark before the leader arrived. He came riding in through the narrow opening on a large black horse, masked, dressed in dark expensive clothing, heavily armed, and obviously very much in control. His eyes quickly took in the entire amphitheater. He almost immediately noticed Raider. "What the hell is that man doing here?" he demanded, his voice whip-sharp.

Jackson immediately moved forward. "It's okay, boss," he said quickly. "I brought him."

The man remained on his horse, looking down at Jackson. "You brought him?" he asked incredulously. "You brought a stranger *here?*"

"I checked him out real careful, boss. An' you know we lost Buck our last time out, so we were short a man, an' I thought . . ."

The boss swung his eyes off Raider and onto Jackson. "If I wanted you to think," he said coldly, "I'd have let you know. Didn't I get it through your head that I'm the one who picks new men, and only me, and that's the only way we can keep any of this from coming back to rest on any one of us? Didn't I tell you that?"

"Well, uh, yeah, boss, I suppose that's what you said. But I'm tellin' you, I checked this one out real good. Hell, he's even got a price on his head, and he's a real good man with a gun."

"I don't give a fuck if he's another Jesse James," the boss snapped. "I don't know a damned thing about him, that's what counts with me. Who the hell are you, mister?" he demanded, looking straight at Raider.

Raider felt the impact of the other man's eyes. They were of an intense blue, accentuated by the dark mask through which they looked out at the world, as cold a pair of eyes as Raider had ever felt lock onto him, and he knew that if he didn't satisfy this man, he was probably very close to cashing in his chips. "The name's Raider," he said curtly. "And I *am* a good man with a gun."

The other man continued to hold his gaze. Raider made it a point not to look away. Finally the other man nodded. "Okay," he finally said. "It's done. You're here. You can ride with us, but if you foul up in any way, if you give me any cause to be unhappy with you, then you're a dead man. Understand?"

Raider nodded. The boss swung down from his horse and headed over toward the fire. "I'd like something to eat," he said curtly.

One of the men by the fire quickly moved aside and pointed to the stew pot hanging over the fire. Hard as these men were, when this unknown boss gave an order they obeyed it with amazing speed. He must be quite a man, Raider thought, to build discipline into this bunch. Even Jackson, who was as murderous and independent a man as Raider had ever met, had been sweating blood when the boss tore into him a few minutes earlier. The only one who had not seemed to react to him at all was Ernie Duval. But then, Raider considered Duval a special case, a man so obsessed with killing that he noticed little else.

Raider circulated among the other men while the boss ate. It soon became clear from their conversation that this was the only name they knew him by. The boss. He was a medium-sized man, perhaps a little toward the tall side, with a trim, whipcord body. But it was not his physical presence that one noticed; rather, it was the dynamism of his personality, the hard merciless strength that radiated from him. Once those cold blue eyes fastened on a man, it was hard to think, and harder to act.

The boss got up from the fire, wiping his mouth on an expensive-looking handkerchief.

He's used to money, Raider decided. He grew up with it.

"Gather round," the boss called out. The men began to drift in toward the fire. When they had formed up around him, the boss said flatly, "We're hitting a mine this time. Payday is coming, and they have a big work force, which means a lot of cash on hand. There's maybe a hundred thousand dollars waiting to be paid out, most of it in gold. We ride in fast, wipe out any opposition, grab the money, then ride out as fast as we rode in. We divide the money our usual way, then split up. Any questions?"

Jackson was the only one who spoke up, perhaps because he was nettled by the way the boss had spoken to him, and he now wanted to make his weight felt a little. "Yeah. Which mine we hittin'?"

The boss looked at Jackson for several long seconds. "You really amaze me," he finally said. "You know that, except for myself, none of us are to know the objective until we're ready to hit it. You know that we do it this way so that nobody can shoot off his mouth and give the game away before we've really started playing it. So why the hell are you asking, Jackson?"

"Well, I—"

"Fine. Now, let's get a couple of hours' sleep, and then we ride."

Raider noticed the sullen look on Breaker Jackson's face as the men drifted to their bedrolls. But he also noticed that Jackson held his peace. Raider headed toward his bedroll with the others, trying to pass as close as he could to the boss without attracting too much attention. He tried to see beyond the mask, to fit the other man's features into his memory, looking for some outstanding characteristic that would make future identification easier, but he couldn't get past those hard blue eyes, which were suddenly looking in his direction. "Thanks," Raider said, thinking it best to say something. "Thanks for letting me in on this."

The boss came up to him. "Just remember what I said before. If you give me even the slightest reason to doubt you, you're a dead man."

Raider nodded. The boss turned away and went over to his own bedroll, but even though he lay down, Raider suspected that the other man wasn't sleeping. The last of the light died, and the sound of snoring sounded gently in the clear dry air, on the surface a peaceful scene, but in reality, a prelude to robbery and murder.

# CHAPTER FOUR

They rode out a little after midnight. It took the boss a while to kick most of the sleeping, cursing men out of their bedrolls, although Raider was up and ready to move at once.

It was a fine night, the sky clear, as it usually was this time of year. Since there were no lights to compete with them, nothing man-made, the stars spread across the sky in fantastic profusion, the Milky Way was a broad band of shimmering light. The moon was not up yet, but the starshine was enough to guide the ten men through the rough landscape.

Raider wasn't happy with the situation. He hadn't meant it to turn out this way, actually riding out on a raid with bandits. His mission had been to locate them, particularly to locate their leader, then guide a party in to destroy them. Raider, like the harness mender, was a longtime operative of the Pinkerton National Detective Agency, working undercover. The wanted poster had been fabricated by his employers, to give him stature in the eyes of bandits. However, the poster, to boost its authenticity, had been widely

circulated. Raider had not been joking when he'd told the
harness mender that some bounty hunter might try to collect his head for the reward.

If only he'd been able to get a message to the harness
mender. But the boss's careful planning had made that impossible. For now he'd have to go along with the fiction
he'd created, that he was a desperado. Eventually, he'd
grab the first chance he had to take out the boss.

They rode all night. Raider had to hand it to the boss, he
kept good order among the men, forcing them to set a good
pace, and most importantly, not to fight among themselves.
They were a murderous bunch, as much in danger from
each other as they were from the law.

The moon came up in the early hours of the morning,
bathing the rugged landscape in a ghostly white light. They
were able to make better time now, and the boss pushed
them harder. He'll pay for all this disciplining someday,
Raider thought. These are not the kind of men who take
well to being ordered around.

The darkness faded, the eastern sky brightened, and
soon the sun came up, cheering the tired men—until the
day began to grow hot. Grousing and complaining intensi-
fied. Finally, at noon, the boss called a rest, the men gratefully dismounting and seeking out shade; but the boss
forced them to take care of the horses first. "You're going
to need them to ride to safety," he insisted. "If they're not
in good shape you could end up dead or in jail."

Raider was increasingly impressed by the boss's sense
of organization and leadership. He wondered if he might
have at one time been in the Army. Or if he still was. The
erect, alert way he sat the saddle suggested a cavalry background. He'd sure as hell like to know more about the
man.

After an hour's rest they pushed on, but when they
began to spot an occasional cabin the boss ordered them to
ground. They holed up for the rest of the day in a small
draw. Most of the men immediately lay down to catch up
on their sleep. Those who did not were ordered by the boss
to do so. "It's going to be a long night," he warned them.

They were on their way again as soon as it was dark enough to ride unseen. They rode until one o'clock in the morning, when the boss finally called a halt. As usual, the horses were his first concern, the men coming a distant second. "Bed down," he ordered, "And keep the noise low. The mine is just the other side of the hill."

When he was certain that the men had made an adequate camp, that they were reasonably safe from discovery, the boss called Breaker Jackson over. "We'll do some scouting, you and me."

He looked over at Raider, hesitated a moment, then added, "You come along too."

The boss insisted that they do the reconnaissance on foot. Raider and Jackson cursed under their breath as their high-heeled riding boots slipped and slid over the rocky ground. Neither man had much love for walking, but they knew that in this case it was necessary. The ground was so rough, broken and steep that horses would have been a hindrance.

They finally reached the top of a rocky crag. The boss lay down next to a huge boulder and looked over the edge. "There it is," he said in a low voice.

Raider moved next to him. The mine was about half a mile away, and maybe five hundred feet lower than their position. It was a big mine and obviously a busy one. Lights burned everywhere. The minehead was particularly well lighted. Even from this far away they could see men coming and going from the large clapboard structure that had been built over the pit. "They have both a night shift and a day shift," the boss said. "We'll want to be going in just after the day shift goes down the hole."

Raider nodded. Here was another example of the careful planning characteristic of the boss. They were to make no move against the payroll until the maximum number of potential defenders were down the hole, far out of the way. True, the night shift would be aboveground, but they'd be half asleep, slow to react.

The moon was up now. The boss used its light to sketch a rough map of the area around the mine. He had obviously never been here before. Raider wondered how he knew so much about the payroll and about the mine operation.

Satisfied, the boss led Raider and Jackson back to the camp. "Get some sleep," he ordered the two men. "We saddle up at dawn."

Raider headed toward his bedroll, which he'd placed in the deep shadow of a huge boulder, in the hope that he might be able to slip away during the night and alert the mine personnel. He saw that Duval had spread his bedroll not far from his own. Duval was lying in the bedroll, but he wasn't asleep. Raider saw the white gleam of the other man's teeth as Duval grinned at him. "Boss's orders," he said.

So, the boss had posted a man to watch him, and Duval was making no attempt to hide his function. There had never been much love lost between Raider and Duval. Raider loathed Duval and didn't care if the other man knew it. Duval had similarly open feelings about Raider. So there would not be much chance of slipping away to warn about the raid.

Raider slept as much as he could, awakening from time to time to see if Duval had drifted off to sleep. Perhaps he did sleep from time to time, but whenever Raider moved, Duval seemed to come awake, his teeth glinting again in that same strange, mocking smile.

The boss routed them out just before dawn. A few minutes were allotted for a quick cold breakfast, then the horses were saddled and bridled, bedrolls and gear strapped into place, weapons checked, and finally it was time to move out. The boss broke the men up into three groups, each group riding down toward the mine by a different route. The boss had picked out the routes in the moonlight the night before, choosing each one for the cover it offered. He had done such a careful and thorough job that the bandits arrived at the mine unseen, and all at the same time.

Events began to speed up. "You and you," the boss snapped to two men, "take up covering positions in the direction of the mine head." Two more men were detailed to cover the opposite direction. Another man was to hold the horses.

That left Raider, Breaker Jackson, Ernie Duval, and one other man to go along with the boss when he hit the mine office, where he assured them the payroll money was being kept. Before going inside the boss turned to Raider. "Give me your pistol," he ordered. Raider hesitated, wondering if right now might be the best time to resolve the whole thing, the time to draw his .44 and either make an arrest or kill the man. But he was aware of Breaker Jackson and Ernie Duval standing right behind him. One wrong move and they would certainly gun him down. "You'll get your piece back if you need it," the boss said, his hand on the butt of his own pistol. "Until then . . . let's just say that you're on probation."

Raider had little choice. He nodded, then slowly pulled the big Remington out of its holster, twisting it in his hand so that he was able to offer it to the boss butt-first. The boss took it, thrust it into the waistband of his pants, then jerked his chin toward the mine office. "Let's go," he said curtly.

They moved in fast, striding straight up to the office door. A man walked around the corner of the building, barely noticed the bandits at first, then gawked at the boss's mask. Breaker Jackson hit the man over the head with his pistol barrel. The man went down with a startled squawk of fear and pain. Jackson hit him again and he was quiet.

The boss opened the office door and stepped inside, followed by Raider, Jackson, and Duval. The fourth man stayed behind to guard the doorway. The interior of the office consisted of one large dusty room, with small dirty windows set into two of the walls. There were two clerks inside. They looked up in annoyance as the four men came into the room, their annoyance turning to consternation as three of the men drew pistols and covered them. "The payroll," the boss snapped. "We want it, and we want it fast."

"But . . ." one of the clerks protested. Breaker Jackson

rushed toward him and hit him on the side of the face with the barrel of his pistol, the front sight slicing into flesh. The clerk staggered backwards, blood running down his face.

"I said we want it fast!" the boss repeated in a deadly voice.

"It's . . . in the safe. Locked up," the dazed clerk burst out.

"Then open it," the boss snapped.

"The . . . the combination . . . it's . . ."

"Don't try to lie to me," the boss said coldly. "I know that you know the combination."

"No. I swear I don't."

The boss turned away in disgust, then motioned Ernie Duval forward. "Convince him," he ordered.

Duval grinned. His knife was suddenly in his hand. He walked toward the dazed and bleeding clerk. Light flashed on the long blade. "Wait . . . wait . . ." the clerk started to say, but Duval had already cut him before he'd finished speaking, a shallow groove across the chest, leaving his shirt gaping open, the long painful cut slowly oozing blood.

The knife went up against the man's face, the blade lying flat against his cheek, the razor-sharp tip less than an inch from his left eye. "You make the boss wait any longer an' I'll take out your eyeball," Duval hissed.

The cold feel of the knife against his cheek, the burning pain of the cut across his chest, but most of all, the crazy, gleeful look in Duval's eyes decided the clerk. "Don't! Please don't! I'll open the safe! I'll open it!" he babbled.

The safe was back in a corner, half hidden by a temporary wooden partition. It was a big safe, black, with enameled printing across the front of the door and gold striping around the sides. The boss jerked the clerk away from Duval, then pushed him to his knees in front of the safe. "Get to work," he ordered.

The clerk began spinning the big dial. After a few turns he looked up nervously. "I missed it that time," he said apologetically.

"Don't miss it the next time. It may be your last," the boss warned drily.

"It's just that I'm so nervous . . ."

The dial began to spin again. The safe was the natural focus of attention, but Raider let his gaze move around the room. Out of the corner of his eye he noticed what he hoped the others did not notice—the second clerk, who was partly out of the line of sight, slowly moving his left hand back toward a heavy cord that came out of the ceiling and dangled down the wall next to one of the desks. There was a wooden handle on the end of the cord to give purchase. Raider watched the man's fingers grope for that handle. Raider had a pretty good idea where that cord led. He tried to move to the side, to screen the clerk from view, but he wasn't in time. Just as the safe door swung open—the clerk by the safe having been more successful with the combination this time—the clerk standing by the wall boldly seized the handle on the end of the cord and tugged hard.

Outside, a whistle began to shriek loudly. The boss spun around. He immediately realized what had happened. "You stupid idiot!" he screamed, the first time so far that Raider had seen him lose his usual cool control. His face contorted with rage, and he jerked his pistol from its holster and shot the clerk through the head. The man flew back against the wall, screaming, both hands pressed against his shattered skull. The cord swung free, but the whistle continued to shriek wildly, repeatedly, like the howling of some huge wounded beast.

The boss spun back to the safe. The remaining clerk was watching in horror as his companion thrashed out the short remainder of his life on the office floor, his brains seeping out through the hole in his skull. "Get moving!" the boss shouted, leveling his smoking pistol at the clerk. He signaled to Breaker Jackson, who tossed a large canvas sack onto the floor next to the safe. "Put all the money in it," the boss demanded.

From where he was standing Raider could look straight into the safe. It was packed with greenbacks and heavy-

looking bags of gold coin. He looked back toward the man
dying on the floor only a few yards away. If only he had
his pistol!

The remaining clerk began stuffing money into the sack,
urged on by the boss. The whistle continued to scream.
Jackson and Duval were looking around nervously. Suddenly shots thundered outside. The man guarding the door
backed into the room. "One hell of a lot of men coming
this way!" he shouted.

"Hurry!" the boss bellowed to the clerk, who had by
now shoveled most of the money into the bag. The gunfire
outside began to intensify in volume. One of the men who
had been posted outside came running into the office. "We
gotta get the hell outta here!" he shouted. "There must be
two dozen men with guns out there. An' the night shift is
comin' outta their bunkhouses, an' about half of 'em got
guns."

"Order the horses brought around to the side of this
building," the boss snapped back at him. He kicked the
clerk aside, then scooped up the bag, staggering a little
under its weight. "Come on," he said to the men remaining
with him. "Time to ride."

As he said this, the man guarding the door suddenly
flew backward into the room, a hole in the front of his
shirt. The boss ran to a window, drew Raider's .44 from
his waistband, smashed the glass with the barrel, then
emptied the pistol out the window. Howls of rage and pain
sounded outside.

The boss tossed Raider the empty pistol. "Come on,
let's get moving!" he shouted, drawing his own pistol and
running out the door.

Raider, Jackson, and Duval followed him out into the
open, where all hell was breaking loose. A group of miners
had taken cover behind a building about fifty yards away
and were pouring fire in their direction. The boss and the
men with him returned the fire. Raider suddenly realized
how vulnerable he was, standing there beside bandits with
a pistol in his hand. It was an empty pistol, and he wasn't a

bandit, but the miners didn't know that. They were trying to kill him along with the bandits.

The bandits who had been left outside on guard were huddled behind a building, firing back effectively, giving cover to the man who was bringing up the horses. The horse holder was riding hell for leather, lying flat on the back of his mount, the reins of the other horses held tightly in one hand. By the time he made it to the shelter of the building, he was white as a sheet, but unhit.

"Mount up!" the boss snapped.

Immediately the survivors swung up into their saddles. There were nine of them left, including the boss. The man who'd been hit in the office had been left for dead.

The remaining bandits made a dash for it, the boss launching them straight at a group of miners who had been running toward their cover. The miners yelped, snapped off a few shots, then wisely sprinted for cover. One of the running men was hit in the back and fell heavily. Ernie Duval, yelling jubilantly, slipped off his horse with easy grace, knelt for moment, cut the wounded man's throat, and was back up in the saddle almost immediately.

A howl of rage went up from the mine's defenders; Duval's action had been performed in plain view of everyone. A number of armed men came running out from behind cover, firing madly at the bandits. The man next to Raider was hit. Raider could hear the meaty smack of the bullet plowing into flesh; he could hear the man's shocked grunt of pain. The wounded man reeled in the saddle and almost fell, but another of the bandits rode in close and propped him up, whipping the wounded man's horse with his own rein ends, urging the terrified animal into a run.

They went racing away from the mine, riding madly, a couple of the men turning to fire parting shots back at the mine defenders. Raider rode with the rest, bent low, hugging his saddle, aware of bullets whizzing by overhead and on both sides. Being a Pinkerton wasn't going to help him now. Bullets were not capable of making distinctions.

"They're gettin' horses!" Breaker Jackson shouted. "They'll be on our trail in a couple of minutes."

Raider twisted in the saddle. Sure enough, men were mounting up back at the mine head.

"Jesus Christ! They're gonna catch us!" one of the bandits screamed.

"Shut up and ride," someone else snarled.

But the wounded man was slowing them down. He was reeling in his saddle, unable to control his mount. The man who'd helped him before kept trying to steady him, but without much success.

The boss ordered a halt, rode close, looked at the wounded man. "Leave him behind," he ordered curtly.

"Uh-uh," the man who'd been helping the wounded man snarled. "Jake's my buddy. I ain't leavin' him nowhere, not while he's still alive."

"Well, then, what the hell?" Duval cut in, grinning lopsidedly, reaching for his pistol with the obvious intention of finishing off the wounded man. The man's friend immediately made a move for his own pistol.

"Stop it!" the boss snarled, moving in and placing the muzzle of his pistol against Duval's head. "No fighting among ourselves. How many times do I have to tell you?"

Duval, still grinning, obediently slid his pistol back into its holster, but Raider sensed, from the intensity of the light coming from Duval's slitted eyes, that he was probably mulling over the possibility of shooting the boss in the back the moment he turned away.

A good chance for Raider, who was furiously shucking the empties out of his Remington and stuffing in fresh shells. There had been no opportunity to reload back at the mine; he'd had no choice but to run for his life with the others, but maybe now he could get the drop on the robbers while they were stopped and hold them until the men from the mine caught up to them.

The wounded man suddenly fell from his horse. His friend dismounted to help him just as a mob of riders came pounding around a bend about two hundred yards back along the trail. The men around Raider lashed their horses into motion and a moment later were all pounding along

the track, leaving Raider no choice but to race along after
the others, unless he wanted to completely lose touch.

The wounded man and his companion were left behind.
The wounded man had managed to rise to his knees, and
his companion was vainly trying to get him up on his feet.

And then the pursuers were on them. The unwounded
man tried to throw his pistol away, but was cut down by a
fusillade of shots. Raider, looking back over his shoulder,
saw it happen. Damn, those miners were sure as hell quick
on the trigger . . . didn't give the poor bastard much of a
chance to surrender.

Raider slowed down a little, still looking back. He saw
the pursuers gather around the wounded man, who had
fallen over onto his back again. Guns were raised, half a
dozen of them crashed out, their bullets pounding the
wounded man down into the dirt.

Goddamn! They'd shot him in cold blood! But . . . why
the hell not? Raider realized. The miners had seen Ernie
Duval get down from his horse and slit a wounded miner's
throat. They were obviously not in a forgiving mood, they
were out for revenge, an eye for an eye. Besides, their
payroll had been stolen. There would be no wild Saturday
night in town this week. Any of the bandits who got caught
would be lucky to be shot down at once. The rest would
end up swinging from the end of a rope thrown over the
nearest tree limb.

Which ended any hopes Raider might have had of join-
ing forces with the mine's defenders. To them, he was just
another of the men who'd killed their companions and stolen their wages. He'd never live long enough to explain
who he was. He now had no choice other than getting the
hell out of here with the boss and the others—or die very
quickly.

# CHAPTER FIVE

Having the best horse, Raider quickly caught up with the others. They were riding recklessly, hell bent, trying to put as much distance as possible between themselves and the posse of angry miners. And now Raider received a surprise. The boss, who had so far shown incredible coolness, was obviously as badly rattled as the others, riding frantically, crouched low over his horse's neck, his eyes wild. Well . . . so the bastard wasn't perfect after all.

For Raider, the problem was going to be how to get out of this with his neck unstretched. He rode up alongside the boss. "If you keep pushin' the horses this way, they're gonna play out."

The boss's head jerked toward him. "What the hell do you suggest? That we slow down to a walk and let them catch up to us?"

"That's what's gonna happen if we keep poundin' along like this. Their horses are fresh. Ours have been ridden hard for more than two days. We've gotta play for time."

Ernie Duval had ridden up close. "Big talk. Let's hear some ideas."

42

Raider took a quick look around at the countryside. It was rugged, not as broken as the Jackson Hole country, but rugged enough. "We gotta slow 'em down," he said. "Those rocks up there . . ."

About five hundred yards ahead, the trail began to climb up toward the heights where they had camped the night before. Huge boulders jutted up alongside the point where the trail began its climb. "We'll get some men up in there," he said, pointing toward the rocks.

Breaker Jackson understood immediately. "Great idea. We'll blast 'em out o' their saddles."

Raider nodded, although he wanted to make sure that didn't happen. He meant to save his neck, but he had no intention of killing men he had been hired to protect.

The bandits pulled up behind the rocks. Some of the horses were already badly lathered. "You take most of the men on ahead," Raider said to the boss. "Just leave me two men with rifles. That should be enough firepower to shake 'em up; they're miners, not gunfighters. You take it slow for about half an hour, then stop to rest the horses. The three of us should be able to hold 'em off for at least that long."

The boss gave him a long searching look. He seemed to have gotten himself under control again. "It's a good plan," he finally said. "But in the future, when you get an idea, clear it with me first."

"Right," Raider said, nodding. Humor the bastard. The important thing was to get out of this alive.

The boss detailed two men to stay with Raider. They looked scared. One of them started to complain, but the boss shut him up with an icy look. Raider suspected that only the most expendable of the men were being chosen for this rear guard, which category undoubtedly included himself. That was fine with him. He wanted men with him that he could control. He was delighted that he hadn't been left with Jackson or Duval.

The rest of the men rode off at a slow canter while Raider and his two men clambered into position high up in the rocks. They were barely in time. The posse came pounding around a bend about five hundred yards away. Raider positioned the two men behind rock outcroppings, rifles pointed down-trail. "Aim for their horses," Raider ordered.

"What the hell for?" one of the bandits demanded. He was a rat-faced man with buck teeth.

"Because they're an easier target, shithead. Just do what I say."

The pursuers were now within four hundred yards. Raider raised his big Winchester, sighted down the long barrel, fired. The leading horseman's mount reared up, pawed the air, fell heavily, the rider barely able to leap clear in time to keep from being pinned. The animal's dying scream echoed up into the rocks.

By the time it had fallen, Raider had fired again. Another horse went down. The two men with him commenced firing, their bullets kicking up dust about fifty yards ahead of the posse. "Too damned far," Rat-face snarled. A second later Raider brought down a third horse. "What the hell you shootin' with?" Rat-face demanded.

"Winchester Centennial. .45-75. Shoots almost as far and as hard as a Sharps."

Raider's next shot missed, mostly because the horsemen below, seeing the havoc being wrought amongst them, had the sense to swerve and race for cover. Raider's companions whooped excitedly and began to fire madly, kicking up more harmless dust. "Careful you don't waste ammo," Raider snapped. "We may have to be here awhile."

Silence fell, except for distant sounds of cursing from where the possemen had taken cover. Now they began to fire back at the rocks, but, like Rat-face and his companion, their lighter-caliber rifles, mostly Winchester seventy-threes, which were for the most part chambered for pistol cartridges, could not quite reach their target. Raider knew they would try to work closer. He would use the longer range of his big Centennial to force them to keep their distance. The three horses lying out in the open were warning enough. Raider noticed that one of them was still kicking feebly. He put it out of its misery with a head shot.

"Jeez!" Rat-face half whispered under his breath.

It now ceased to be a battle and became a game of maneuver. The possemen were doing their best to work closer, to try to circle around behind the rocks and cut off the defenders. Raider and his two men were doing their best to keep them pinned down.

Raider, knowing that his advantage would eventually succumb to the posse's greater numbers, began preparing his exit. Leaving the other two men to keep up a slow but noticeable fire, he scrounged the area, eventually finding several dead tree limbs straight enough for his purpose. Pulling out his bowie knife, he lopped off any twigs or protuberances, cut the limbs down to a length of about four feet, then rolled them in the dirt to make them a uniform color.

When he returned to the others, he noticed a flicker of movement off to the left. Somebody was trying to flank them. He lay on the ground, carefully sighting his rifle. He fired, saw a hat fly away among the bushes below, heard a man yell in fright. He fired again, kicking dust into the man's face, and now the man was running full-tilt for cover.

That should hold them for a while. Raider looked up at the sun and calculated that they had already delayed the posse more than half an hour. He pulled his two men back, then laid the sticks he had cut into place, pointed down at the flats below, hoping they would look like rifles. "Okay," he whispered to the others. "Let's get our asses out o' here real quiet-like."

The two gunmen had been certain at first that they were going to be sacrificed so that the others could escape. They were more than glad to be leaving. The three of them slipped down the back side of the rocks, took the reins of their horses, and led them quietly up the trail. They didn't mount until they were more than a hundred yards away. Behind them, they could hear the possemen still firing off an occasional shot. Good. If the miners made enough noise it might take them a while to realize that no firing was coming back at them from the rocks.

"That may hold 'em for another ten minutes or so," Raider said. "Let's make tracks, but try not to push your horses too hard."

They caught up with the others an hour later. They were riding along sedately, their horses looking rested. Raider's mount was still in pretty good shape; the rest back at the rocks had helped. The two men with him had shown themselves to be good horsemen; their mounts were in relatively good shape too.

The boss extracted a description of what had happened from Rat-face and his companion. He then nodded toward Raider. "Good work."

"Thanks. Now let's get lost."

The boss nodded again, his face expressionless behind the mask. "Suppose you show us how."

"Glad to oblige."

For the next few hours, Raider used every bit of trail craft he knew to shake himself and the others loose from the posse. He led the way up streambeds, leaving the water only when he judged the ground was hard enough to hide tracks. For several miles they followed a small horse herd, losing their tracks in with the herd's tracks, although a good tracker should be able to pick the marks of shod hooves from the tracks left by the unshod wild ponies. Raider eventually rode close enough to spook the herd, which caused the animals to run off in all directions, which he hoped might confuse any trackers.

By nightfall they were sprawled on the ground on a high plateau, resting their horses again. The boss was lying on his stomach, studying the trail below through a pair of large binoculars. "I think you've done it," he called out to Raider. "Take a look."

Raider came over and took the glasses. Following the boss's pointing finger, he studied the land below. Yes, there they were, about a mile away, the posse, milling about in confusion at a point where the trail split five ways. He could imagine the heated arguments flying back and forth between those men, as each put in his say as to which route their quarry had taken. Finally, they turned down one of the five trails, the one leading directly away from where the bandits were hidden. Raider smiled. "Yeah. I figured that'd be their choice."

"You mean you planned that, too?" the boss asked.

"More or less. I'd noticed some hoofprints leading off that way. We were already above the main trail. It seemed sensible that they'd follow the only tracks they could see. I didn't figure they had anybody with them good enough at tracking to realize those prints were over a day old."

Duval's voice cut in, cool, mocking. "Got us a real injun scout here, boys."

Raider turned around, looked back at him. Duval met his gaze for a moment, then casually looked away. I'm going to kill that little son of a bitch someday, Raider promised himself.

There was now little fear of further pursuit. The seven survivors of the mine raid pushed on toward their hideout in the Jackson Hole country, reaching it the second evening of their flight, the men exhausted, some of the horses nearly dead. Most of the men flopped onto the ground, too tired to even spread out their bedrolls. Solidly back in control now, the boss ordered that a guard be set. Raider wondered what had brought on that strange panic at the beginning of their flight. Obviously there was a certain degree of instability in the boss's makeup. A strange man.

Raider offered to stand guard. The boss hesitated, then finally agreed. He trusts me now, Raider thought. Why not? I saved his skin today.

No one had the energy for splitting up the loot, so it was put off till the next morning, when a rested and eager group gathered round as the boss tossed his big canvas bag down onto the ground and knelt to untie the cords holding it closed. The bag had not left his possession since it had been stuffed with money by the terrified clerk in the mine office.

The bag held more than thirty thousand dollars. The boss counted out more than three thousand apiece to each of the men. His take was in excess of thirteen thousand dollars. One of the men had the temerity to complain about the size of the boss's cut. The boss's head came up, the cold bright blue of his eyes pinning down the complainer. "Good planning comes expensive," he said icily. "If you don't like the way we cut up the money, then say so and get out."

The man hesitated, then nodded. He, as well as the rest of the men, knew that the only way out of this outfit was on a slab.

Of course, the complainer was not the only one resentful of the boss's larger cut. Fully aware of the prevailing mood, the boss broke the tension by counting out a further thousand dollars each to Raider and the two men who'd stayed behind with him to slow down the posse. "Extra risks bring extra money," the boss said curtly. The fact that the extra danger money had come out of his own cut defused the general resentment. "Okay," the boss said. "Let's separate until the next time."

The men immediately began to prepare to leave. Raider realized that this might be his best chance. If the boss was one of the last to leave the hideout, that might be the time to take him. Instead, he was almost the first to ride out. Raider tried to think of a good excuse to follow him, but could not. Jackson and Duval were already saddling up. "Come on," Jackson called out jovially. "Fork your nag and let's ride for town. We got us a hell of a lot of money to spend."

Raider had little choice but to ride with them. By the time they left the hideout, there was no sign of the boss, not even any sign of the direction in which he'd headed; his tracks were obscured by the tracks of other men who'd already ridden out, and with Jackson and Duval alongside him, Raider knew that he couldn't make a big show of interest in the boss's whereabouts. He did, however, on the long ride back to town, use every bit of trail sense he could command to not only fix the location of the hideout in his memory, but also to analyze the countryside for good ambush spots. Among other things he noticed that for the first couple of miles there was only one possible route leading away from the hideout. The gang would always have to take this route on the way to or from a raid. Valuable information.

The ride back was an annoyance. Ernie Duval was becoming increasingly difficult, pushing Raider verbally, always just the easy side of too far, needling the bigger man, trying to goad him into a mistake of judgment.

Raider considered the possibility of having it out with Jackson and Duval right now, here on the trail, just drawing his gun and telling them that they were under arrest. He could either take them in or, if they resisted, kill them. The gang had lost three men on this raid. Two more lost would weaken it considerably.

But that would blow his cover, and Raider knew that the real center of the gang, its heart, was the boss. Without him, the gang would be nothing but a bunch of disparate, inefficient gunmen. Even if he wiped out every member of the gang except its leader, the gang would spring up again, forming around the boss with new members but with the same heart, the same cool, organized head.

The only way to destroy the gang for good would be to cut off that head. The boss was obviously a master criminal. Take him out, and the gang would crumble away. Leaderless, the various gang members would drift apart, shoot off their mouths, fall into errors of planning, end up in jail or dead. No . . . he would have to bide his time. He would have to wait until he had a good shot at the boss.

# CHAPTER SIX

The closer they got to town, the more jovial Breaker Jackson and Ernie Duval became. Their pockets were full of money, and they were planning how to spend it. Jackson's taste seemed to slant toward whiskey, gambling, and women. Duval seemed mostly interested in women. Raider had an uncomfortable time imagining this cold-blooded little killer with a woman. He remembered how Duval had gutted the man in the bar two weeks before, and how he had cut the wounded miner's throat only yesterday. Ernie Duval was a man who genuinely liked to hurt people, a man, in Raider's book, who needed killing himself.

Once they were back in town, Raider headed for his hotel, while the other two headed straight for the saloon. Raider led his horse around to the stables behind the hotel. The stable boy, Jimmy, was seated on a hay bale, playing mumbledy-peg with a broken barlow knife. He leaped up when he saw Raider. "Hi, mister. Say, your horse looks real done in. You musta rode him one hell of a long way."

This boy will make a detective someday, Raider thought sourly—if he ever learns to keep his mouth shut. "Yeah, a long way. Get his saddle off, brush him down, and give him some oats."

"Sure."

Raider had started to walk away, but now he turned back to face the boy. "Say, did that harness mender bring back my spare bridle yet?"

"Uh-uh. He was gone for a while, but I think he just got back into town. He's probably out at his usual place, over by Pap Johnson's. You want I should go over there and get the bridle back for you?"

"Nope. I'll get it myself later."

Raider went up to his room. There was a chipped water pitcher on the commode. He looked inside. It was half filled with scummy water, which hadn't been changed since he'd left. He tossed the water out the window, took the pitcher downstairs to the washhouse pump, and filled it with fresh water, with the intention of taking it back upstairs and washing his face and upper body. The sight of a huge old claw-footed bathtub in a corner of the washhouse changed his mind. "Pritchard!" he called out.

He had to call again before there was any movement from inside the hotel. Finally, preceded by the sound of grunting and the shuffle of feet, Pritchard came into the washhouse, head low between his shoulders, as usual, buzzardlike, looking suspiciously up from under his brows at Raider. "Yeah?" he grunted.

"A bath. What does a man do to get a bath around here?"

"Bath?" Pritchard said, surprised. "You want a bath?"

"Yeah. In that tub over there. A hot bath."

Pritchard eyed Raider as if he might be suffering from sunstroke. Every intelligent man knew that bathing was bad for the health, that a too-liberal use of water washed the natural oils out of the skin, that it could lead to fever, croup, even consumption. Pritchard himself had not taken a bath for the past three months; his smell was proof of it. But, on the other hand, if a man wanted to live recklessly, well, Pritchard was willing to be liberal-minded—and also willing to make the usual profit. "Hot water'll cost you fifty cents."

"Fill up the tub."

Pritchard nodded, walked to the door that led to the rear of the hotel, stuck his head outside, and delivered the inevitable bellow, "Jimmy! Where the hell are you, boy? Get your lazy ass in here!"

The boy seemed to materialize out of nowhere, panting a little, either from being out of breath, or from fear of his employer. "Yeah, Mr. Pritchard?"

Pritchard jerked his head in Raider's direction. "This gent wants to take a bath. Heat some water and fill up that old tub."

Jimmy's eyes grew wide. He looked back and forth between Raider and the tub, as if having difficulty believing that a man who was so obviously all man, like Raider, would want to do what Pritchard had said he wanted to do. But maybe there was something to this bath stuff that he was missing, some secret that he didn't fully understand. He took another look at Raider. Yep... all man. Jimmy kicked around the idea of maybe taking baths himself, maybe even a couple of times a week. Smiling as if he'd made a great discovery, one he shared only with his friend Raider, the boy dashed out of the room.

While Jimmy was heating the water, Raider went upstairs to get his one change of clean clothes. Half an hour later he was back in the washroom, luxuriating in the big tub, steam rising around him, the hot water soaking the trail aches out of his muscles. Jimmy had been kicked out the door, clutching another quarter as if it were a twenty-dollar gold piece. And now Raider began to plan how he would destroy the boss and his gang.

An hour later, washed, dried, changed, and shaved, Raider approached the shack where the harness mender tended to hole up when he was in town. Raider found him sitting outside on a flat rock. When he saw Raider approaching, the harness mender raised a hand in lazy greeting, then went into the shack and came out holding Raider's mended bridle, which he handed to him.

"Took you long enough," Raider growled.

The harness mender hunkered down on his rock. "Oh, it was finished a coupla days ago. But you wasn't around to collect it."

Raider hunkered down across from him. "Nope. Out for a little ride."

"Yeah? Well, that little ride wouldn't have nothin' to do with a certain mine payroll robbery, would it?"

Well, as a matter of fact, it just might."

"You were there?"

"I was there."

The harness mender nodded his head slowly, looking pensively down at the ground. "Lotsa dead bodies outta that one."

"Too damned many."

"We gotta stop those bastards."

"You don't say?" Raider replied somewhat sarcastically. "Well, I'll tell you, they're a hard nut to crack. The bastard that leads 'em is smarter'n hell. Plans everything down to the last little detail."

"You met him?"

"Yeah. He was wearin' a mask. I don't think any of his men know who he is."

"So we're no closer."

Raider shook his head. "Oh, we're close enough. I think we can bust 'em wide open. Now, here's what I figure we should do . . ."

The two men talked for another fifteen minutes. Finally, Raider decided that spending any more time with the harness mender would be an unnecessary risk. He picked up his bridle and wandered back to his hotel. There would be nothing to do for the next few days except wait.

Fortunately, Breaker Jackson and Ernie Duval left town early the next morning. There was a conspicuous lack of available women in town, so the two bandits headed for the nearest settlement with a large enough stable of whores to satisfy their needs. They didn't return for more than a week, looking somewhat the worse for wear. It wasn't difficult to tell, from their general air of surliness, that most of the money they had earned in the mine robbery was already gone.

While they had been away whoring, Raider had had another meeting with the harness mender. He showed up alongside Raider one night when he was on his way to the saloon, materializing with an unnervering abruptness. The two men quickly slipped into the dark mouth of a stinking alleyway. "I found it all right," the harness maker murmured. "It was just like you said—only one way in or out."

"You think it'll work?"

"Don't know what else would."

"Good. Then wait for my signal."

The harness mender melted away into the darkness. Raider didn't notice him around town again for several days, which was almost too late, because Breaker Jackson approached Raider in the saloon one night, just a day after the harness mender had returned. "Like to make some more money?" he asked.

"Yeah."

"Good. There's a raid on. We leave in an hour. Get your gear."

Obviously Raider was more trusted now; Jackson permitted him to go to his room alone to collect his gear. Raider filled his saddlebags quickly, prepared his bedroll —and carelessly hung his dirty shirt in the window frame. He knew, considering the lack of service in Pritchard's hotel, that the shirt would not be removed.

He, Jackson, and Duval were on their way well within the hour. As they rode out of town, Raider made as much noise as he thought he could get away with, wanting to hedge his bets by using more than one way to alert the harness mender. The signal of the shirt in the window might be enough, but then again, it might not.

It was the usual day-and-a-half trip to the hideout. Every mile of the way, Raider was mentally calculating what must be happening behind him. If the harness mender had indeed seen his sign, knew that the gang was about to make another raid, certain events should now be in motion. The harness mender had personally scouted out, following Raider's directions, the land lying around the hideout. A large party of Pinkerton operatives had been stationed within a day's ride of the hideout for the past week. The harness mender would ride like hell for the nearest telegraph office, send them a message, and the Pinkertons would be on their way to the spot where they would ambush the bandits when they left the hideout.

The timing was somewhat thin-stretched. First, the Pinkertons had to be able to reach the ambush site in time. Raider had estimated that the Pinkertons would have more than forty-eight hours after he left town with Jackson and Duval to get into position, since it would take about thirty hours for the three of them to reach the hideout, another few hours for the rest of the gang to filter in, then a night of rest before leaving. Forty-eight hours, give or take a little. Barely enough time to set up the ambush.

As before, Raider, Jackson, and Duval reached the hideout late in the afternoon of the second day. Many of the gang members were already there, and surprisingly, the boss was already there too. He gave Raider and his two companions one quick irritated glance, then looked back toward the hideout's entrance. "Where the hell are they?" he muttered, referring to two men who had not shown up yet. "It's past time we got moving."

"We're leaving right away?" Raider asked, surprised.

"Yes. Within the hour. Why? That bother you?"

It bothered Raider very much. If they left now, instead of during the night or in the morning, the ambushers wouldn't have time to get into place. "It's just that I was hopin' we could get a little rest," he said to the boss.

"This isn't a knitting bee, Raider," the boss said testily. "Timing is of the essence in this operation. We'll have to move out on schedule, whether we're all here or not."

Three men had been lost in the last operation. Raider noticed four new faces. Obviously the boss had done some recruiting. There would be a total of ten men if everyone showed up. Too many men to handle by himself, and that would be his only alternative unless he could find some way to delay their departure. He tried to think of a workable plan, perhaps laming a horse or two, but he didn't see how he could accomplish it without getting caught. He could lame his own horse, of course, but then they would probably simply leave him behind.

The two missing men arrived half an hour later. "Okay, mount up," the boss ordered. There was a great deal of grumbling as the men swung up into their saddles; Raider was not the only one who had indicated a desire to get some sack time. Raider had no choice but to go along with the others. To hang back now would probably cost him his life.

There was no ambush. They rode past the ambush point without incident. All that Raider could do was to ride at the rear of the little cavalcade and do his best to leave the broadest trail possible. If he left enough sign, maybe the Pinkerton posse would be able to follow the gang. He knew they'd have old Charlie Hendrys with them. Charlie had been a scout and tracker for the cavalry during the Indian campaigns. Before that he'd lived many years with various Indian tribes. But could Charlie follow a trail through land like this, and at night? It would be dark soon, and judging by the boss's haste, they would be riding until very late.

The boss called a halt a little after midnight, more to rest the horses than to rest the men. The stop was a short one, only two hours, and then they were on their way again, pushing on until an hour past dawn, when the boss led them into the shelter of a small wood overlooking a sizable town, which lay about a mile away. "Rest up, boys," he said, pointing down toward the town. "We'll be down there in a little while . . . robbing the bank."

The men gratefully dismounted, the more intelligent among them unsaddling their mounts, rubbing them down, then feeding them a small ration of oats, not enough to founder them, but enough to give them energy if speed was needed later. As it probably would be, once they'd robbed the bank.

Like any good commander, the boss let the men know a little about the operation, so that they would feel a part of it. "We have to hit the bank just as it opens," he explained. "They have a time lock on the vault, so hitting it any earlier wouldn't do us much good. I also happen to know that the local sheriff will be out of town this morning—a request he got to investigate some stock shortages clear over on the other side of the county."

"I guess we know who sent him that request," one of the men said with a grin.

The boss actually favored him with a smile. "Through channels he'll never be able to follow. Anyhow, we'll hit the bank hard and we'll hit it fast. In and out in fifteen minutes, that's the way I have it planned. Now . . . any questions?"

"Yeah," Raider cut in, more to slow things down than for any real curiosity—he kept thinking of the Pinkerton agents following behind on their trail, if indeed they were actually following. "How much cash do you figure there is in this bank?"

"About a hundred thousand dollars," the boss said coolly. Several of the men whistled. A hundred thousand dollars was one hell of a lot of money.

"You sure?" Raider asked.

"Yes, I'm sure, the boss replied, with an acid edge to his voice. "I have ways of knowing."

Raider silently wondered just what those ways might be. The boss had known how much there would be at the mine, too. And he had also known some of the details of the inner workings of the mine office. Just who was he, anyway, that he could know these things?

They mounted up at exactly nine o'clock, all ten of them, and moved in a compact body toward the town. There was no point in trying to slip into town in small groups, unnoticed. The mask covering half the boss's face was enough of a giveaway, so they rode in boldly, walking their mounts until they were within sight of the town's inhabitants; and then on the boss's orders they all put spurs to their mounts and rushed the bank.

It was the usual well-planned operation—a man to hold the horses, four more fanning out around the bank, facing the street, rifles and pistols in their hands, ready to hold off any attempts by the town's citizens to defend their bank. Clear in every bank robber's mind was the way the James-Younger gang had been shot up, virtually destroyed, by a group of angry citizens, when Jesse James and Cole Younger and their various brothers had hit a Minnesota bank.

The remaining five men, including Raider, ran into the bank, pistols in hand. "Up against the wall!" the boss shouted, pointing his pistol at two customers. The customers stared, openmouthed, and when one moved a little too slowly, the boss fired his pistol into the floor near the man's feet. Stinging splinters flying into his shins gave the man wings; he raced over to join the other customer by the wall, his hands held high over his head.

A clerk tried to make it out the back door. Breaker Jackson shot him through the right leg. The clerk fell, cursing and howling, rocking back and forth on the floor, holding his bleeding leg.

It was the usual clockwork operation, three of the bandits running from till to till, stuffing canvas bags with money, while the boss and Ernie Duval herded the clerks, along with the fat, sweating, obviously terrified bank manager, into the vault, for the real money.

In far less than the fifteen minutes the boss had specified, they had collected all the money worth taking. "All right! Everybody into the vault!" the boss shouted, indicating the customers, the clerks, and the bank manager.

"But there's no air in there," the manager whimpered.

"That shouldn't bother you. You'll stay outside while we lock them in. You can work the combination and let them out while we ride away."

A good enough plan. The bank manager would be occupied with saving his customers and clerks while the gang made good its escape. The prisoners were herded into the vault, minus the manager, who stood wringing his hands next to the vault while the boss slammed shut the heavy vault door and spun the dial. "Don't start opening it until you hear us riding away," he ordered the manager, who nodded dumbly. "Okay, let's hit the trail!" the boss shouted to his men.

They were just striding toward the door when they heard the sudden sound of firing from outside in the street. "Speed it up!" the boss shouted, racing for the door.

When they got outside, the men who had been left on guard were hunkered low next to the horses, shooting down the street.

"What is it? What's happening?" the boss demanded.

"Some citizens . . . holed up in that hotel down there. Started shootin' at us. I think we hit one, which oughta keep their fuckin' heads down."

"Good enough. Now mount up, and let's head out of town in the opposite direction."

A heavy covering fire from two bandits who had good cover next to the bank slowed the rate of fire from the hotel. Raider swung up into the saddle beside the others, cursing inwardly. If only the boss didn't plan everything so goddamn well, he could take on the gang from within their ranks, while the townspeople kept them in disarray with the weight of their fire from the hotel.

But it wasn't working that way. So far, not a bandit had been hit. The bandits' fire was very accurate. Raider saw windows exploding all along the side of the hotel as the bandits' bullets tore into the building. Now almost no one was firing back at them. All they had to do was ride on out of town in the opposite direction, which they proceeded to do, the boss leading the way.

Then suddenly one of the bandits gave a cry of alarm. "Jesus Christ!" he screamed, pointing toward a horde of heavily armed horsemen, who were thundering into town from the direction in which the gang had hoped to flee.

Raider's Pinkerton posse had arrived at last.

# CHAPTER SEVEN

There were between fifteen and twenty of them, all heavily armed, all hard, well-trained men, and they were coming on fast, firing rapidly. The boss openly flinched away from them, ready to turn his horse and race away in the opposite direction. But in that direction lay the hotel, and the armed townsmen within.

And now, just as at the mine, when events had seemed to go against him, the boss once again showed signs of panic and indecision, first sitting his horse woodenly, obviously not knowing what to do, then losing control completely, sawing on the reins, spinning the animal in a complete circle, his head darting first in one direction, then in another.

It didn't help matters when the fat little bank manager, who had seemed so ineffectual during the robbery, suddenly appeared on the sidewalk in front of the bank, holding an enormous shotgun. "Rob *my* bank, will you?" he screamed, and proceeded to unload both barrels into the nearest bandit. The man was blown right out of his saddle, the entire left side of his body reduced to a bloody froth.

His weapon now empty, the bank manager prudently darted back into the relative safety of the bank to reload.

The boss, apparently recovering his powers of decision, suddenly spurred his horse into an alley next to the bank. Breaker Jackson and Ernie Duval and one other man rode hard after him. Meanwhile, saddles were being emptied around Raider as the posse's fire took effect. Several horses were down, their riders, some of them wounded, taking cover behind the fallen animals, firing back desperately at the posse.

"Goddamn it, they're getting away!" Raider cursed under his breath as he watched the boss and the men with him pounding madly down the alley. He spurred his horse after them, reaching down to pull his rifle from its scabbard, and then he was nearly knocked from the saddle as something hard and hot struck him a tremendous blow in the ribs. He reeled, barely hanging on, feeling a hot stickiness spreading down his side.

He'd been hit! Probably by a bullet from the posse. There was too much shooting going on for the Pinkertons to be able to pick and choose their targets. It had been his responsibility to get the hell out of the way once the shooting started, but, worried that the boss might escape, he'd waited too long.

Tightly gripping the thick barrel of his horse's body with his legs, he clapped spurs to the animal and took off down the alley after the fleeing bandits, reaching across his body with his left hand, pressing hard under his right arm in an attempt to slow the flow of blood.

There they were ahead of him, still four of them, including the boss, heading toward a maze of corrals and stock buildings, obviously a holding area for cattle about to be shipped out of town. Raider tried to reach down for his pistol, but his right arm wasn't functioning well. He had to concentrate all his strength just to remain on his horse's back.

And then, about a hundred yards ahead of him, he saw the boss reel in the saddle and nearly fall off the far side of his horse. He'd been hit too! The boss righted himself with difficulty, one of the men riding alongside pushing him erect. Raider urged his horse forward. He had to catch up!

The fleeing bandits disappeared into the maze of buildings and equipment at the far end of the alley. Raider took a quick look behind him. The downed bandits were blocking the alley mouth, fighting desperately against the possemen, unknowingly keeping them from pursuing the others—including the boss, Jackson, Duval, the men who had abandoned them.

Raider could not expect any help. He continued to drive his animal onward, and, turning a corner, saw the four men ahead of him, still riding hard, leaving the last buildings behind now, heading for a patch of woods about a mile from town. Raider doubted that the possemen could see them.

Riding hard, Raider finally caught up to the others inside the little wood. But what the hell was he going to do now? The numbness was fading from his right side, replaced by pain. He could barely move his right arm.

"Raider!" Jackson shouted. "You made it out."

"Yeah," Raider replied, his left hand still clamped against his right side.

"He's hit too," Duval said.

"Not too bad," Raider murmured, although he didn't know if he believed it himself. He rode closer, wanting a better look at the boss. The masked man was still in the saddle, but the entire back of his shirt was soaked in blood.

Ernie Duval dismounted and motioned to Breaker Jackson. "Help me get him off his horse."

With the help of the fourth man, they got the boss dismounted. He grunted with pain, his eyes half glazed, but he seemed to be doing his best to cooperate.

Duval took out his knife and cut away the boss's shirt. There was a small bluish hole high up on the wounded man's back, slowly welling blood. Working with amazing speed, Duval cut up part of the bloody shirt for a compress, pressed it against the wound, then wound the rest of the shirt in long strips around the boss's body, holding the compress tightly in place. "Now you," Duval said, motioning to Raider, who was still sitting his horse.

Raider slid to the ground, grunting from the pain the movement cost him. Duval tore at his shirt, examined his ribs. "Nothin' much. Bullet hit you at an angle, bounced off a rib. I suppose it hurts like hell, but it ain't likely to kill you."

He called Jackson over and motioned toward the boss, who was sitting on a rock, slumped against a tree. "He's another story," he murmured. "Bullet's still in there. He could check out on us. Either way, he's gonna slow us down. What do you say? Do we take him with us or leave him here?"

Jackson hesitated, but finally he said, "We oughta take him along. He knows who we are. If the law gets their hands on him, we could be dead meat."

"Not if he ain't alive to talk," Duval insisted.

Jackson scratched his head thoughtfully. "Well, I dunno, Ernie. We been makin' a lotta money workin' with that hombre. If he stays healthy, we could make a lot more."

"He ain't makin' us much this trip," Duval groused. "When he got hit he dropped those two big money bags he was carryin'. We only got the two little ones left. Maybe a few thousand bucks."

"That's why we gotta keep him alive. So's we can get more."

"Well, okay. But if he looks like he ain't gonna make it . . ."

So much for honor among thieves. It would make things a lot easier for Raider if they dumped the boss right now, but it didn't look like that was going to happen. Not at the moment. Raider's biggest hope was that the possemen would catch up to them soon. Although he was wounded and hardly in any condition to take on superior odds, he might be able to disrupt the surviving gang members just long enough to cause them to be captured or killed.

Once again, he found himself tagging along. Duval had bound up his wound, which was hurting like hell now, which he figured was a good sign. He kept flexing the fingers of his right hand, wondering how his body would take to the heavy kick of his .44. Surely the posse would be onto them soon.

But it failed to show. Hour after hour they rode, with no sign of pursuit. Raider remembered that they had cut across the stockyards. The ground there had already been churned up by a mass of hoofprints, both of horses and of cattle. Even old Charlie Hendrys would have trouble picking out their sign.

And then, late in the day, it began to rain, very hard, a real gulley washer. Looking back along their trail, Raider saw their own tracks being quickly washed away. While it was still pouring down rain, Breaker Jackson led them off the main trail and up into the mountains. Not too much chance of their being tracked now.

The boss was having a hard time of it. On three separate occasions Duval called a halt, at which time he helped the boss dismount, checked his bandages, and poured water down his throat. By now the boss was only half conscious. He made no complaint when Duval took off his mask, the better to give him water. Studying the boss's naked face, Raider supposed he could be called a good-looking man. He had regular, strong features, quite pleasant except for those hard cold eyes, which were partly glazed now. Clearly, the man hardly knew where he was.

He had guts, though. Each time he was hoisted back up into the saddle, he hung on with grim determination. They rode throughout the afternoon and into the night. Raider, growing somewhat light-headed from loss of blood, lost track of time. He hardly knew what was happening when the little band of tired men finally ended its journey. He faintly remembered being helped into a small, dirty, seemingly abandoned cabin. He saw his bedroll being spread out on the floor, sank down onto it, and a moment later was asleep.

He awoke at dawn, his right side aching fiercely. He lay still, eyes only half open, and in the dim light saw Breaker Jackson and Ernie Duval bent over a form stretched out on the cabin's only bed. Turning his head slowly, Raider saw that it was the boss. Jackson and Duval were speaking in low voices, but Raider was able to make out what they were saying. "That bullet's gotta come out or he'll die," Duval insisted.

"So take it out," Jackson replied.

Duval snorted. "That'd kill him for sure. I ain't' no doctor."

"You two—stop wasting your time arguing."

The voice, weak, hoarse, but speaking with its usual authority, had come from the prone figure on the bed. Raider saw the boss's head slowly turn toward Jackson and Duval. "Duval's right. I need a doctor. Get me one and you get five thousand dollars apiece."

Jackson and Duval glanced at one another, interest lighting up their features. Jackson thought for a moment, looked back at the boss, then nodded. "Okay," he finally said. "There's a town about half a day's ride from here that I'm pretty sure has a sawbones. I'll find him and bring him here."

"How you gonna convince him?" Duval asked.

Jackson grinned, hefted the big Colt in the holster by his side. "I'll think of a way."

A few minutes later Jackson was gone, leaving Duval behind to do what he could for the boss.

Raider groaned, pretending that he had only just awakened. "Jesus," he grunted, gritting his teeth as he sat up.

"Stiffenin' up a little, ain't it?" Duval asked, grinning. He made no move to help as Raider slowly got to his feet. Raider walked over to the boss and looked down at him. His eyes were closed at first, but then they opened and he looked up at Raider. "You're still with us," he said, sounding a little surprised.

"Sure. What else?" Raider answered. But instead of replying, the boss closed his eyes again and seemed to drift off into either sleep or unconsciousness.

Raider shrugged, met Duval's look, then went outside. The other man who'd made it away with them was outside, sprawled on his bedroll, asleep. Raider tried to remember his name. Hank, that was it. He was named Hank. A rather stupid man, brutal, a bully and a coward, if Raider had judged him right. He woke up blinking owlishly at Raider. Raider wondered if now might not be the time to act, take out Hank, and then go into the cabin after Duval, who was alone in there with the boss, who was probably too badly wounded to put up much of a fight.

But Raider himself was having so much trouble moving his right arm that he wondered how effective he himself would be. If he made any noise taking out Hank, then Duval would be on him at once. Maybe it would be better to wait until Jackson got back anyhow. He wanted Jackson, too. So, hearing running water, Raider followed the sound to a small, clear stream. He took off what was left of his shirt, unwound Duval's bandages, then took a look at his wound. It was ugly, a long deep gouge in his side, along the ribs, probably not dangerous as long as he kept it clean, but it felt as if maybe a rib or two had been cracked when the bullet richocheted off him. Making any kind of fast move—hell, moving at all, even breathing—wasn't easy. He wasn't certain he could even hold a pistol. Yeah, better hold off any showdowns until he felt a little better.

Raider wadded up his shirt, dipped it into the water, then began cleaning his wound. The icy water stung like hell. He gritted his teeth and kept on sponging away dried blood until he was satisfied he'd gotten it all clean. Then he wandered around awhile until he found his saddlebags. There was a clean shirt inside, and some old pieces of cloth. He used the pieces of cloth for a fresh bandage, then put on the shirt. He felt better now, but exhausted. Working on his wound had worn him out, no doubt he'd lost quite a bit of blood yesterday. He went back into the cabin, picked up his bedroll with his left hand, carried it outside into the sun, spread it out on a bed of pine needles, then lay down on it, resting, letting the hot sun beat against his wounded side, taking the ache out of his muscles. After about half an hour he fell asleep.

# CHAPTER EIGHT

Jackson returned with the doctor just before dark. The doctor didn't look too happy about this particular house call; it was obvious from his manner that Jackson had kidnapped him at gunpoint. He was a middle-aged man, very competent-looking. When he was taken into the cabin to see the boss, any hesitations or resentments he might have been feeling suddenly dropped away from him, replaced by an urgent professionalism. "This man should have seen a doctor a long time ago," he snapped at Jackson and Duval.

"Well, ya see, Doc," Duval snickered, "we didn't really know if there was any doctors with the posse."

The doctor began rapping out orders, which Duval and Jackson seemed somewhat hesitant to follow. Raider stepped in, fetched water from the stream, and heated it to the boiling point on the little wood stove inside the cabin. This doctor was apparently one of the ones who'd taken to the relatively newfangled practice of sterilizing his cutting instruments.

He had ether with him, but the boss at first resisted the idea of being unconscious while someone worked over him

with sharp implements. The doctor shrugged, then began
probing for the bullet with the boss still conscious. The
agonizing pain—the bullet was very deep—soon convinced the boss of the value of an anesthetic, so the doctor
placed a few drops of ether on a piece of cloth and held it
over the boss's mouth and nose. The boss coughed and
wheezed for a few seconds, then went limp. Now the doctor was able to probe for the bullet without the wounded
man making the job more difficult by writhing beneath the
knife.

The doctor worked over the boss's unconscious body for
more than half an hour. After fifteen minutes the bullet was
out. The doctor held up the bloody, misshapen piece of
lead, looked at it, then dropped it into a tin dishpan. It
landed with a loud clank. Even with the bullet out, the
doctor felt it necessary to cut away some of the flesh
around the wound, which had already had time to mortify.
"We don't want to save him from the bullet and then have
him die from gangrene," he explained to the watching
men.

Next it was Raider's turn. The doctor examined his
wound, nodded, then said, "I see you've been taking good
care of it. Nice and clean; no signs of infections."

He spread some salve on the raw flesh, which stung.
Raider felt good enough about it. He knew from prior experience with wounds that he would feel fine within a few
days. The doctor straightened up. "Now, can I go home?"
he asked Breaker Jackson.

"Don't be an idiot, Doc. We can't let you go until we're
ready to leave here ourselves. An' I don't hardly see him"
—he gestured toward the boss's unconscious body—"sit-
tin' a horse for some little time yet. Do you?"

"No," the doctor admitted. "He'll be a pretty sick man
for at least a week."

"Well, the sooner you get him well, the sooner you can
mosey on home. Understood?"

"Understood," the doctor said woodenly, nodding his
head.

For the first two days after the doctor had taken the

bullet out of him, the boss remained unconscious the greater part of the time. He woke occasionally to ask Jackson or Duval how things were going, and if there were any signs of pursuit. At first there weren't, then, after Jackson had ridden out one day to bring in supplies—their small stock of food was getting very low—he came riding back up to the cabin in the late afternoon, sweating, his horse lathered, obviously very much bothered. "God," he said to Duval in a low but intense voice. "The whole damned area down in the flats is swarmin' with posses and lawmen. Lookin' for us, I kinda think."

"The doctor. It must be because of the doctor. They probably missed him by now, figure we mighta dragooned him. Jesus, we gotta get outta here."

"Uh-uh. We gotta wait. What about him?" He jerked his head toward the cabin, where the boss was still convalescing in bed.

"The hell with him. We got our own necks to save."

"Yeah. But we're broke, an' he still owes us five thousand bucks apiece, enough so's we can live pretty high on the hog, if we can make it down into Mexico. He ain't gonna give us that money till we get our asses outta here, his included. Besides . . . ain't nobody gonna find us in here. Not unless they know where the place is."

Jackson had a point. The cabin was situated in a small box canyon, invisible from the outside, and tricky to reach even if you knew where it was. As long as they stayed quiet and out of sight, they would probably be able to avoid detection. Raider was painfully aware of that.

Raider also began to become aware of a definite danger to his health. One day he was sitting outside in the sun in front of the cabin. Hank was sitting a few yards away, keeping an eye on the doctor, who was down at the stream, washing out bandages. Jackson and Duval were inside the cabin, holding a conference with the boss, who was by now much improved. Seeing that all of Hank's attention was on the doctor, Raider got up and moved noiselessly around behind the cabin, slipping along the back wall toward the cabin's sole window. The window had at some time in the past contained a pane of glass, but it had long ago been broken, leaving only a few dirty shards at the bottom of the window frame, so that he had little difficulty overhearing what was being said inside.

"The doctor's got to go; we can't let him leave here alive," a voice said. It was the boss's voice, as cold and as commanding as before he'd been wounded. "He's seen my face. I can't be sure, but I think there's a chance he might have recognized me. And if he hasn't, he might run across me someday, and then it would all come out."

There was the sound of feet scraping against the gritty cabin floor. "I'll go out an' take care of him right now," Ernie Duval's voice cut in.

"No. Not yet. Not until we're sure I don't need him any more."

"Okay. It can wait, then."

There was a slight pause, then the boss's voice sounded again. "There may be something else that will eventually have to be taken care of. Raider. I know I don't really have anything concrete to go on, but ever since he came into our operation we've had nothing but trouble. I can't believe it was just a coincidence, all those men showing up when we were hitting the bank. Somebody had to have tipped them off."

"Hell," Breaker Jackson cut in. "I can't see how that was possible. I was watchin' him all the time. He didn't have no chance at all to tip anybody off. An', like you planned it, none of us, includin' him, knew where we was goin' except you."

"Nevertheless, he could have found a way. What do you really know about him? I remember you saying that he was a wanted man."

"Yeah. I saw the poster when I went through his stuff. The Pinkertons are offering five hundred bucks for him."

"The Pinkertons?" the boss burst out. "It was a Pinkerton wanted poster?"

"Yeah. The real McCoy."

"Jackson," the boss said icily. "There would be nothing

easier than for the Pinkerton Agency to fake a wanted poster."

"You think he's a Pink?" Jackson burst out.

"I don't know. It's only a possibility. But, considering what's happened to us since he joined up . . ."

"Goddamn it. I'm gonna go out and kill the bastard right now."

Again, the scrape of boots against dirty wood. "Hold it, Jackson," the boss cut in. "I only said there might be a chance that he's a Pinkerton. Anyway, he wouldn't be as easy to take as the doctor. Unless I miss my guess, Raider is one hell of a dangerous man. There might be shooting, and that's the last thing we want right now. If there are, as you say, posses hunting for us in this area, shooting would bring them right to us."

"Well, what're we gonna do?"

"Just wait. He's not going anywhere. When I'm strong enough to travel, that's when we'll get around to the question of what to do about Raider. And the doctor, too. In the meantime, we'll keep a sharp eye out. No trouble, no fighting until then. Is that understood?"

"Okay, okay," Jackson agreed sullenly.

"Good. Now you two go outside and send Hank in here. I want to talk to him."

"Hank?"

"That's what I said. Hank."

"Jesus. That asshole has been bitching his guts out 'cause we took in so little money from the bank robbery."

"He won't be complaining after he and I talk. Now send him in."

Raider heard the clump of boot heels heading toward the door, then Breaker Jackson called out, "Hank? Get your ass in here. The boss wants to have a little palaver with you."

Raider was still pressed against the rear wall. With Jackson and Duval outside in the front there was a chance he'd be discovered. He decided to chance it. He was curious to hear what the boss might have to say to Hank— shiftless, lazy, not-too-bright Hank, who, he would have thought, would be the last of the men the boss would want to confide in. Besides, what did he have to lose? It sounded like he was already living on borrowed time. If they discovered him here, listening, it would only mean that the inevitable showdown would happen now instead of later. He'd almost welcome that. What worried him most, however, was that if he were killed or run off, that would leave the doctor without anyone to help him get out alive. He'd have to do his best to see that the doctor got his chance. This was the coldest bunch of killers he'd ever run across.

He heard Hank clomping into the cabin. "You wanted to see me, boss?" Hank asked.

"Yes, Hank, I need your help on an important mission." The boss's voice was brisk, businesslike.

"Me?"

"Yes. I need someone to carry a message for me. To my wife. As far as she knows, I'm on a short business trip. I was to have returned home today. What worries me is that she might panic if I don't return, and report me missing. I can't have that, there would be questions, and in the light of the recent robberies, some people might start to wonder. Do you understand?"

"Ah, yeah. So you want I should tell her you're okay. Not to get all shook up."

A moment's silence, a growing sense of exasperation in the boss's voice. "I tell her that myself, Hank, in a note. You're to take it to her. Privately. No one must see you talking to her. Just give her the note. You don't really have to say much of anything."

"Yeah . . . sure," Hank replied a little sullenly.

"There will be something concerning you in that note, Hank."

"Yeah? What?" Now Hank sounded a little nervous.

"Ten thousand dollars. That's what I intend to give you for doing this for me. There will be instructions in that note ordering my wife to send a bank draft, a sight draft, to a certain bank in a certain name. When we go pick up that money, Hank, you and me and the others, ten thousand dollars of it will be yours."

"Goddamn!" Hank burst out. "Ten thousand dollars!"

"Right. Just make sure my wife gets the note. Here. I've already written it. Can you read, Hank?"

"Yeah. A little."

"Her name and address is on the front."

There was a rustle of paper, some mumbling from Hank, who was obviously sounding out a name and address, but too softly for Raider to make out the words. "Cheyenne, huh?" Hank finally said.

"Yes. Now, get on your way as quickly as you can. It should take two days to ride there, two days to ride back. Don't waste any time. I want you back here four days from now. By then I should be in good enough shape to ride. Then we'll go pick up your ten thousand dollars. Understood?"

"Sure, boss. I'll be gone in fifteen minutes."

Hank stomped out of the cabin, obviously in a hurry, no doubt very excited by the prospect of sudden wealth. Raider, suspecting there was no more to be heard, and no good reason to stretch his luck any further, slipped quietly away from the cabin, traveling in a big circle, so that when he came in sight of the cabin again he was approaching from the opposite direction. Hank was already saddling up, and within another five minutes had ridden out, his face set, his dim brain no doubt fixated on the idea of that ten thousand dollars.

Which Raider doubted he'd ever live to see. If his mission was successful, he'd be the only one among them all who knew who the boss actually was, and the boss sounded like a man of substance, one who would not want anyone to be able to connect him to the recent string of robberies. No, the most Hank could logically expect when he returned was a bullet in the back. But then, Hank was not long on logic, which, no doubt, was the reason the boss had sent him.

Apparently the boss was planning a wholesale slaughter once he was well enough to ride: Raider, the doctor, and

Hank. This might be the time to act, to take them on before they got him from behind. He could simply take off, of course, but that would be leaving the doctor in their hands, and he knew he couldn't do that. And besides, he would be leaving without really knowing who the boss was.

As it was, leaving did not turn out to be that easy. The horses were kept penned up right next to the cabin, in plain view of all. It would be very difficult to get to his horse and ride out, and without a horse he knew he'd be ridden down within a few miles. There was always the chance, of course, that the boss's suspicions would lessen, that he and the others wouldn't turn on him. But he couldn't count on that.

Over the next three days Raider did his best to stay out of the way, to act as if he knew nothing of their plans or suspicions. It was on the fourth day that he knew he'd have to finally act, because that was the day Hank was slated to return. Already the boss was well enough to leave the cabin and sit out in front in the sun. True, he was still a little weak, and in a certain amount of pain, but he obviously had an iron constitution and was healing extremely quickly. The doctor was amazed by his patient's rapid recovery, apparently unaware that when the wounded man was fit enough to ride, his own life would come to an abrupt end.

On the morning of the fourth day, Raider finally got his chance. Breaker Jackson had been guarding the doctor, but he eventually became bored. "Raider, you take over for me," he said. "I got some things to do."

Raider nodded his agreement. He suspected that what Jackson had planned was a visit to a bottle he had stashed away. He watched Jackson disappear up the little box canyon above the cabin. The boss was inside sleeping, and the last he'd seen of Ernie Duval, he'd been down by the stream tossing pebbles into the water.

He and the doctor were alone. "Well, this is our chance, Doc," Raider said in a low voice.

The doctor had been sitting disconsolately on a rock.

Now his head jerked up. His expression mirrored suspicion. "What are you talking about?"

"Time to get the hell out of here."

"I don't understand."

"You don't think they're gonna let you live, do you?"

"I was wondering about that. But why are you . . . ?"

"I'm not one of them. I'm a Pinkerton agent, a ringer. I got myself planted here to help bust up this gang, but it ain't worked out quite the way I figured. I think they're gettin' onto me, and it's high time I hustled my ass outta here. Yours and mine both."

"I . . . I was having a hard time fitting you in with them. They're going to kill me, you say?"

"Yep. Heard 'em talking about it. Now, you ready to light out?"

"I guess I have no choice. But how do we get to the horses. If we go around to that side of the cabin, they'll see us."

"We do without the horses. We light out on foot. But I think we got a good chance of pickin' up a horse down the trail a ways."

"How?"

"You gonna keep askin' questions, or are you comin' with me?"

A second's hesitation, then decision. "I'm with you."

"Okay. Let's go."

It was easy enough leaving the vicinity of the cabin. Walking quickly, they made it out of the little box canyon in fifteen minutes. It was the only way they could go, and this part of their escape threatened the most danger, since, if they were missed too soon, they would be easily found. Farther away, they could strike out in any direction and stand a good chance of avoiding detection.

Luck seemed to be with them. They walked for half an hour without any sounds of pursuit behind them. They were well out of the box canyon now, moving swiftly down a faint trail. Suddenly Raider stiffened. He was pretty sure he had heard the sound of an approaching horseman from farther down the trail. "Get off the path," Raider whispered to the doctor. "Hide yourself in the brush."

"But what about you?" the doctor demanded.

"Shut up and move," Raider snarled. The doctor, nodding, scuttled away deep into the brush. Raider stayed closer to the little trail. A moment later, as he had hoped, Hank came riding into view, his horse lathered, the rider looking only a little less tired.

Raider stepped out into the open.

"Jesus!" Hank burst out, his right hand clawing for his gun. Then he recognized Raider. "Christ Almighty. You scared the shit outta me. What the hell are you doin' down here, anyhow? And on foot?"

"Well, ol' hoss," Raider said lazily. "That's kind of an interestin' story."

"What the hell you talkin' about?"

Raider smiled up at the man. "You didn't really think he was gonna let you live, did you?"

"What . . . what're you talkin' about?"

"Hell, Hank, use your brains, if you got any. You're the only man alive who knows who the boss is, and where he lives. He's busted his gut to keep any of us from knowin' that. You think he's gonna let you go on breathin', takin' the chance you might get drunk someday and shoot off your mouth?"

"How . . . how'd you know I went off to see the boss's wife?"

"He told me. In fact, he gave me an order to come on down here and bushwhack you. He told me about the ten thousand bucks, too, laughed when he said you'd actually believed he'd give it to you."

Hank's jaw dropped. Raider's words rang true. How else could he have known about where he'd been unless the boss had told him? Then the full import of what Raider was saying hit him. "You came down here to bushwhack me?" he demanded, his hand drifting toward the butt of his revolver.

"Relax, ol' hoss. If I'd wanted to bushwhack you, I'd

already of done it, wouldn't I? I wouldn't be standin' here jawin' with you."

"Well then, what the hell . . . ?"

"I don't bushwhack men I've ridden with," Raider said, his voice full of disgust. ''I just pretended I'd do it, 'cause I knew that if I didn't, then it would be all up for me. I think we outta get our asses outta here, buddy. Either that, or go on up there and shoot the hell outta those backstabbin' bastards."

"Yeah . . . yeah. You're right. Ah, goddamn it. I was already countin' that ten thousand bucks. . . . But where's your horse?"

"Couldn't get it away from the cabin. We'll have to double up."

"Double up? Shit, we'd be lucky to get out of here even if we each had the best horse in the world. These mountains are crawlin' with law. They're lookin' everywhere. . . . Jesus, an' to think I risked my neck ridin' back here to warn that double-crossin' son of a bitch. Bigshot banker, is he? I'm thinkin' about goin' on up there an' blowin' his fuckin' head off."

"Banker, you say?"

"Yeah," Hank said bitterly, then he laughed. "Don't that beat all? Here he's been havin' us rob banks, an' he works for one of the biggest banks in Cheyenne. Some kinda big wheel there. Real fancy name to go along with his real fancy job. John Van de Witt. Goddamn Dutchman. He . . ."

Hank's eyes widened. From his vantage point high up on his horse, he was able to see over the brush and quite a ways up the trail. "Jesus, there he is now! Comin' this way, along with Jackson and Duval."

Damn, Raider thought. The men back at the cabin had obviously finally missed him and the doctor, and had come after them. Above, Hank, mouthing obscenities, jerked his rifle out of its saddle scabbard. A moment later a rifle roared out from farther up the trail, the bullet smashing into Hank almost simultaneously. Hank grunted, reeled in the saddle, raised his rifle, got off one shot, and then was hit again. This time the slug knocked him over the rear of his horse. His rifle went flying, hitting the ground not far from Raider. Raider scooped up the weapon, cast one quick glance at Hank, figured that he looked as dead as a man could get, then ran into the brush, heading in the general direction in which the doctor had disappeared. "Doc!" he hissed. "Where the hell are you?"

"Over here."

Raider followed the voice, found the doctor crouched behind some brush. There was very little cover in this area. Standing up would be tantamount to suicide.

Hoofbeats sounded over by the trail. "Hank's dead," Jackson's voice called out. "Now where the hell are Raider and doc?"

"I see tracks goin' off into the brush," Duval's voice cut in. "Let's go in and get them."

"No," a third voice cut in—the boss's. "Let's ride up the trail, get some height. Then we'll be able to see them and pick them off at will."

"Hell, why don't we just ride on out?" Jackson asked.

"We can't leave them alive. I have a feeling that Hank, before we got him, may have told Raider something that he shouldn't know."

"Well hell, let's get it over with, then."

The sound of hoofbeats faded away up the trail.

Raider turned to the doctor and held up the rifle. "Can you shoot?" he asked.

"Hell yes."

"Then take this," Raider said, tossing the doctor the rifle. "And let's try and find us some cover."

He knew the boss had been right, that if they got up above, he and the doctor would be easier to pick off, because there was really no place to hide in this area, just scattered brush, which would give very little cover from the boss's vantage point higher up.

"There they are!" a voice sang out from above. A second later bullets began churning the dirt around Raider and the doctor.

Raider rolled to the side, away from the bullets, into

thicker brush. "Keep moving!" he shouted at the doctor. "Makes it harder for them to hit us!"

He caught a glimpse of Breaker Jackson about two hundred yards above, outlined against the sky, leveling a rifle. Raider blasted off three quick shots with his .44. He saw dirt fly a couple of feet below where Jackson was standing. The range was really too great for a pistol, but at least his bullets caused Jackson to duck down out of sight.

"Over there. I found some rocks," the doctor called out. Raider followed the sound, bullets kicking up dirt around him as he ran. Sure enough, there were some small boulders ahead, just a few, and the doctor was already lying behind them, firing his rifle up at the skyline.

Raider rolled into the cover of the boulders, quickly taking stock of their new position. The boulders were more or less in a line, facing up at the heights. For the moment they were fairly safe.

But not for long. He heard the boss's voice calling out from above, calmly giving orders. "Duval, you go around to the right and flank them. Jackson, you go to the left. We'll have them then."

Damn it, he's right, Raider thought bitterly. Because the rocks were more or less in a line, they only provided cover in one direction. Once Jackson and Duval got into positions out on their flanks, he and the doctor would make easy targets.

Raider tried firing at Jackson as he worked his way around to the side, while the doctor tried the same thing with Duval. But all the other men had to do was stay low behind the skyline and they were relatively safe until they got into firing position.

The firing tapered off. Nobody had any real targets yet, so everyone was saving ammunition. It was in this lull, while Raider was desperately looking around for better cover, that he thought he heard a distant shout from somewhere down below them. He had just about dismissed it as a figment of his imagination when he heard Breaker Jackson call out from above "Goddamn, boss! There's a whole passel o' riders headin' up this way!"

A long stream of curses from the boss. "A posse!" he shouted. "They must have heard the shooting. Come on, boys, we've got to finish off Raider."

"Uh-uh. We gotta get our asses outta here, 'less'n we want 'em shot off."

"No, no. Just a couple of more minutes. Let's finish him off!"

"You finish him off. I'm haulin' ass."

"Me too," Ernie Duval shouted back.

"Goddamn it, *no!* He knows my name!"

"Your name's gonna be mud if you don't get movin'."

Already Jackson's voice was growing fainter. He was obviously running for his horse. Another stream of curses from the boss, several desperate shots sent Raider's way, and then the boss was gone too. A few moments later Raider heard the sound of horses being ridden hard away up the trail.

Raider stood up, raced toward the trail, the doctor close behind him. From below he could hear shouts, the sound of riders approaching. Hank's horse was still standing on the trail, near its late master's body, probably too tired to run. Raider swung up into the saddle. The horse gave a grunt of resignation. A minute later a group of horsemen came pounding into sight, led by a big man on a gray horse. The riders were all armed. Rifles rose to cover Raider. "No. Hold your fire," the big man ordered the men behind him, waving their gun muzzles down. "He's one of ours."

He pulled his horse up next to Raider's mount. "You *are* still one of ours, ain't you, Raider?" he asked, grinning. "We were kinda wonderin' . . . the way you keep ridin' off with those bandits."

"Hello, Will. Yeah, I'm still one o' yours, but three o' theirs are gettin' away over the hill. Let's go after 'em. Just leave a couple of men here to take care of the doc."

The doctor insisted on riding along, doubled up behind one of the Pinkertons. "I intend to manufacture me a gun-shot patient out of one of those bastards," he snarled. "Kidnapping me, planning to kill me . . . they better ride hard and fast."

Unfortunately, the posse's horses were tired from the long haul up from below. So was Hank's mount. Nevertheless, the Pinkertons pushed on, and in another few minutes came to the entrance of the little box canyon. Raider urged the others to slow down. "They may try to bushwhack us," he warned.

But they reached the cabin without incident. A quick look inside showed that the cabin had been hastily stripped of most of the fugitives' belongings. Tracks led away farther up into the canyon. Raider knew of no way out in that direction, but cursed himself for not having made sure earlier. "Come on, let's go after 'em, Will."

The posse continued on up the canyon. The canyon walls began to narrow, rising steeply on either side. It was necessary to ride carefully, always alert for a desperate last-ditch stand by the fugitives. "I think we got 'em, Raider," Will said excitedly. "Looks to me like there ain't no way out."

"Uh-uh. There it is. See?"

Raider pointed to a narrow cleft in the seemingly sheer cliffs rising on either side of the canyon, so narrow a passageway that it would be necessary to ride up it single file. "Mmmmnnn. I sure as hell don't like the looks of that," Will muttered.

"Me neither. We'll have to take it slow, be ready to shoot."

The possemen rode forward cautiously. They had almost reached the entrance to the cleft, the first man ready to ride inside, when Raider thought he heard something, a faint hissing. He quickly looked up. The precipices above the cleft consisted of jagged rock and loose earth. Suddenly he spotted the source of the sound—a plume of gray smoke, spitting sparks. "Back! Get the hell back down the canyon!" he shouted, wheeling his horse.

"What the hell . . . ?" Will demanded.

"Dynamite! They've mined the hillside!"

The possemen all spun their mounts, then went racing

back down the trail. They had ridden about a hundred yards when there was a tremendous explosion behind them. Raider glanced back. Earth and rocks flew high into the air, then came raining back down into the upper part of the canyon. The men pushed their horses on, dodging falling pieces of rock. They rode another fifty yards before they felt it was safe to stop.

A pall of dust hung over the upper end of the canyon. Raider rode toward it. When the dust had settled enough, he saw that the cleft in the cliffs was completely blocked. There was no way a horse and rider could pass. "Well, you got away again, you bastard," he muttered. "But it'll be a different game this time, because I know your name now —Mr. John Van de Witt."

# CHAPTER NINE

The house was large and expensive, and situated in the better part of town on a large parcel of ground. There was a separate carriage house behind and to one side of the main house. A gazebo and a springhouse lay on the other side. Large trees, lawns, and flower beds decorated the property. A banker's house. John Van de Witt's house.

Raider stood outside on the porch, feeling uncomfortable. It was not the house itself that made him uncomfortable, but his intrusion here along with a host of other unwanted visitors.

After Van de Witt, Jackson, and Duval had escaped up the dynamited draw, Raider and the doctor had ridden back down the mountain with Will and the rest of the Pinkerton posse. After dropping the doctor off at his home, Will and Raider wired the Denver office of the Pinkerton National Detective Agency, then rode hard for Cheyenne, changing horses twice along the way, arriving in Cheyenne in the early afternoon of the next day. Immediate inquiries at a local bank about a Mr. John Van de Witt elicited the information that he was indeed an officer of a Cheyenne bank, the largest and richest bank in town. The bank officers whom Will and Raider questioned were at first reluctant to discuss Van de Witt at all with two such dusty, sweaty, tired-looking hardcases. The arrival of James McParland, head of the Denver Western Regional Office of the Pinkerton Agency quickly convinced the bankers to cooperate; McParland was well known and highly respected throughout the West.

"John Van de Witt? You're looking for John Van de Witt?" the president of the bank in which Van de Witt was a vice-president asked, stunned. "Why, John's one of the leading men of our city. Surely there must be some mistake."

"Yeah, his," Raider retorted. "He shouldn't have started robbin' people."

"See here!" the bank president spluttered, trying to meet Raider's icy stare. Raider had very little use for bankers. Or for railroad presidents or captains of industry or executives of any kind. To him they were all worse thieves than even John Van de Witt. Ruthless people-squeezers, covert bandits. "See here?" Raider replied mockingly. "I saw plenty, mister."

"That'll be enough, Raider," McParland said, placing a restraining hand on Raider's arm. Raider started to pull away, then thought better of it. James McParland was not only his immediate boss but was a man he genuinely respected. Tall, heavily built, dressed in a suit and vest with a string tie, wearing round glasses, which did not quite obscure the hard light in his eyes, carrying a heavy walrus mustache above a stern mouth, McParland had not reached his high position in the Agency by sitting behind a desk. James McParland had spent years on the trail, doing what Raider was now doing, pulling in the nation's hardcase desperadoes. He had a reputation for bravery and fair dealing. There were few other men Raider would have permitted to shut him up.

"Mr. Deacon," McParland said to the bank president, his voice conciliatory, "I agree with you. Perhaps there has been a mistake, but charges *have* been made, and I suggest that the best way to clear up those charges is to thoroughly investigate them. Now if you could tell us where Mr. Van de Witt lives . . ."

Sensing the steel beneath the smooth coating of McParland's words, Mr. Deacon complied, giving them the information McParland required. Which information had brought them to the house. And to the woman. John Van de Witt's wife stood uncertainly in the doorway, obviously very confused. "You . . . you want to come into our house? You want to look through John's things?" she asked in amazement, her eyes traveling from one to the other of the large, imposing men standing on her front porch.

"Yes, ma'am," the local sheriff said, somewhat uncomfortably. "We have a warrant."

"But I—"

"I'm afraid you'll have to let us in, Mrs. Van de Witt."

They walked past her into the house. The interior was even more imposing than the exterior. The walls were paneled in hardwoods and decorated with works of art. Fine carpets covered the hardwood floors. Silver cutlery and expensive china gleamed within elegant cupboards and hutches. It was the house of a man who was very well off; to the men seeing it, it was perhaps a little better setting than even a bank vice-president could normally afford.

"I . . . I . . . do you really have to go up there?" Mrs. Van de Witt asked as Raider and McParland started up the stairs to the second floor, while the sheriff and a deputy headed into the parlor and living room.

The upstairs consisted of several bedrooms, a library, and a study. Raider felt like a voyeur as he wandered through these upstairs rooms. He had not wanted to come, but McParland had insisted. "You're the only one except that doctor who knows what the boss actually looks like, Raider."

Raider found the photograph in an upstairs bedroom. It was a luxurious room, dominated by a huge four-poster bed. The photograph was in a gilt frame on a little side table next to the bed, surrounded by articles that obviously belonged to a woman. The connubial bedroom. A loving wife's photograph of her husband.

"McParland . . . in here," Raider called out. McParland came into the room and looked where Raider was pointing —at the photograph. "That's him," Raider said. "That's the boss."

They took the photograph downstairs. Mrs. Van de Witt was sitting on the edge of a chair in the living room, nervously clasping and unclasping her hands. McParland held up the photograph. "Can you tell me who this is, ma'am?"

"Why, what are you doing with that?" she asked sharply. "You have no right—"

"I'm afraid we do, ma'am. Now, if you could just tell me . . ."

"It's my husband, of course." There was anger in the woman's voice. "I don't want you . . . What are you doing?"

McParland had begun prying the back off the frame. "I'm sorry, ma'am," he said. His regret was apparently genuine. Nevertheless, he called over the man he'd brought from the Denver office, extracted the photograph from the frame, handed it to him, then said, "Take this and go out and find a photographer. Have some copies made. Be sure one of them gets to that doctor who was kidnapped, so he can confirm the identification. Make sure another copy goes to our rogues gallery. And one for a wanted poster, of course."

A look of incredulous horror was growing on Mrs. Van de Witt's face. "You . . . you can't be serious," she burst out. "You'll be sorry for everything you've done. My husband is a man of considerable standing and importance in Cheyenne. When he gets back and finds out what you've been doing . . ."

She was interrupted as two small children, a boy and a girl, came running into the living room, closely followed by a distraught nursemaid dressed in a uniform. "Mommy! Mommy!" the little girl cried out. "There's a lot of men in the other room. They're taking things."

The children's voices trailed off as they saw Raider,

McParland, and the other Pinkerton operative. Mrs. Van de Witt drew the children toward her. "See? See what you're doing?" she cried out. "You're upsetting the children!" There were tears in her eyes now. Raider turned away. He definitely did not like this part of the job. He'd rather be facing down the boss, Ernie Duval, and Breaker Jackson, all three face to face, gun to gun, than be here now, destroying this woman.

The sheriff came into the room, holding out a slip of paper. "Is this what you was talking about?" he asked, handing the paper to Raider. It was a receipt for a telegraphed bank draft for twenty thousand dollars, from Mrs. Van de Witt, care of John Van de Witt's bank, to a Harold Swensen, care of a bank downstate. "That must be the money the boss sent Hank for," Raider said.

The men all looked at Mrs. Van de Witt. "John . . . John sent a man here with a note asking me to send that money," she haltingly explained. "John's note said that it was vital to a business transaction he was involved in."

The men stood silently looking at Mrs. Van de Witt. She turned to Raider. "You mentioned the man's name. It was Hank, I'm sure of it. You obviously know him. Just ask him about the note. Can't you do that?"

"No, ma'am," Raider replied.

"But . . . why not?" she demanded, her voice rising.

"He's . . . dead, ma'am."

"Dead? But who . . ." Did you . . ."

"No, ma'am," McParland cut in. "It was your husband. He did it. Your husband killed Hank. He killed a lot of other people, too."

Mrs. Van de Witt had half risen, but now she sank back into her chair, clutching her children close to her. Her face was stunned, vacant. She seemed to want to speak, her mouth moved, but no sounds came out. Raider looked down at the woman, felt a mixture of anger and sorrow. It was Van de Witt who had destroyed her, of course. But why? What in the hell could have pushed a man with all the advantages Van de Witt had to do the terrible things he seemed to have done?

There were no obvious answers. As the investigation continued, a fairly consistent picture of John Van de Witt, his personality and life, began to emerge. He was indeed one of the most respected men in town. In addition to being a bank officer, he was also a deacon in his church, an officer of several civic groups, and a benefactor of local charities.

True, there were some dissenting voices among the nearly universal praise concerning Van de Witt, comments from men with bitter tales of the man's ruthlessness. At first they were written off as the jealous comments of unsuccessful business rivals. But as the probing went deeper, a modus operandi began to appear. Careful digging into Van de Witt's banking affairs indicated that his bank had had dealings with many of the organizations that had been robbed—mines, other banks, express offices, even individuals.

"So that's how he knew all that stuff," Raider murmured when he'd had a chance to look at Van de Witt's banking records. He remembered the boss's considerable knowledge of the internal workings of both the mine they had hit and the bank. Not only had the boss always known how much money there was waiting to be seized, but he'd also been aware of many facets of the inner workings of the organizations themselves. Being a man of such trust, he'd been in a perfect position to gather the kind of inside information that had helped make his raids so successful.

It was Raider who discovered the first really discordant note in Van de Witt's reputation. While McParland and the others continued to investigate Van de Witt's banking connections, Raider began to prowl Cheyenne's seamier side—the saloons and brothels off to the side of the civic center. He went there because he had met Van de Witt on the trail, had had a chance to see into him as a bandit leader, and he knew that there was something inside the man other than the social goodness most of the townspeople had seen.

He found a living reminder of Van de Witt's other side in the person of a hard-bitten but still pretty whore who worked out of a run-down saloon near the edge of town. "John Van de Witt?" the woman said, a bitter little smile twisting the corners of her mouth. "Sure I know him. A real scary son of a bitch. If he hadn't paid me so goddamn much money each time . . . well, cowboy, I'll level with you. He did some things to me I don't even like to think about. Yeah, there was somethin' weird inside that man, all right. Now, I heard the talk that's goin' around town, that he was runnin' that gang that's been doin' all the robbin' an' killin', and I'll tell you the truth—I believe it. Every word. If there's any man around that's made for killin' an' robbin', it's good old John Van de Witt."

The whore had no idea of his probable whereabouts. "I wasn't exactly his bosom buddy," she said wryly. "Though he did kinda like my bosom."

The bank draft Mrs. Van de Witt had sent on her husband's instructions was traced, of course, but it had already been cashed several days earlier. The recipient of the money matched Van de Witt's description, but after receiving the cash, he'd vanished. "A man like him," McParland said sourly, "is probably on his way to Europe or South America by now. I wired all the ports and shipping lines, sent out his picture, too, but so far nothing has come of it. He's either already left the country, or he's lying low, waiting for us to start to forget. I've got a feeling it's not gonna be easy to find him. Unless maybe he's got the other two along. Three men are harder to hide."

"Hard to believe he'd take Jackson and Duval with him," Raider put in.

"Who knows? He certainly has enough money to take along anyone he wants. We checked out his financial affairs, and while he was probably spending a little more than his salary and investments could account for, that still doesn't add up to all the loot the gang made off with. I figure that Van de Witt has plenty of money salted away, enough to buy a lot of safety. His banking background would make it easy for him to know how to hide the stuff."

Raider could only agree. Van de Witt was going to be a hard man to catch. Anyhow, he doubted that he wanted to be a part of the chase, particularly when, on the third day he'd been in Cheyenne, the sheriff brought the bad news.

McParland had been staying at a downtown hotel. He and Raider were conferring there that afternoon, when the sheriff came hurrying in. "It's Mrs. Van de Witt," he said. "She just had some kind of breakdown. Tried to kill herself with one of her husband's straight razors. Cut herself up real bad, not only her arms and her throat, but her face too. God, does she look bad. The doctor says she's gone clear round the bend. He thinks they'll have to maybe put her away in an institution. No tellin' what's gonna happen to those two kids."

Raider turned away, disgusted. "Son of a bitch!" he burst out under his breath. Goddamn John Van de Witt! His bandit games had ruined his wife, an obviously good woman, gentle, well-educated, somewhat innocent. His greed, or whatever it was inside the man that had driven him to a needless life of crime, had destroyed her just as effectively as if Van de Witt had held a pistol to her head and pulled the trigger.

McParland took a critical look at Raider. Raider was perhaps his best operative, particularly when it came to risking his neck in man-against-man confrontations with hardcase desperadoes. This present inquiry was not the kind of thing Raider was cut out for. "How are your ribs holding up?" he abruptly asked.

He was asking about the wound Raider had picked up during the bank robbery. "Huh? Oh, fine. A little sore now and then."

"Look. Why don't you help yourself to a month or so off. Go take it easy for a while."

"Not a bad idea," Raider replied. "Go do some huntin', maybe."

"Bullshit. If I don't miss my guess, you'll be off sparkin' that girl. What's her name? Sarah?"

Raider flushed. "Yeah. Sarah."

"Well just you remember—don't go runnin' off gettin' married like your scallywag partner Doc. We need you."

Raider gave his boss a long hard look. "Can't make no

promises," he growled, then turned and walked out of the hotel.

"Oh, goddamn it," McParland muttered to himself. "Don't tell me I'm gonna lose another man."

# CHAPTER TEN

Raider started for Sarah's house the next day. It was a long journey; Sarah lived in eastern Kansas, about a two-day ride west of Kansas City. Raider could have traveled by rail from Cheyenne, which would have cut his trip down to a couple of days, but, feeling the need for some time to think, he decided to ride horseback all the way. He avoided the towns, such as there were along the way, sleeping out on the prairie at night, usually with his horse's reins looped around his hand, since this was still pretty rough country. Once, in southern Nebraska, he saw a small party of Indians, five of them. They were sitting their horses on a hilltop about half a mile away, watching him. Raider kept on riding. From time to time a few hostiles still rode into the area, from the Dakotas, Montana, and Colorado. However, this band did not bother Raider; they were probably just a bunch of young bucks out looking for some horses to steal. Raider was not particularly worried. It was unlikely that such a small band of Indians would attack a white man as well armed as Raider.

However, in northern Kansas, approaching the Arkansas

River, he became aware that he was being tracked. He didn't really see who it was clearly at first, rather noticed half hidden movement from time to time behind him. Finally, stopping in a patch of brush, he took out his binoculars and studied his back trail. Eventually three men rode out of a small depression, looking down at the ground, obviously following his sign.

Raider was aware that there were white hostiles in these parts far more dangerous than their Indian counterparts, men who would rob and kill travelers for as little as a few dollars. Raider's horse and weapons were a considerable prize. So was the three hundred dollars he had in his pockets.

Raider watched the men through the binoculars until he could make out their faces. Uh-huh. The Simes brothers. He recognized them from pictures he had seen in the agency's rogues gallery. There had been a price on their heads for nearly a year, the result of a long spree of murder, rape, and robbery.

That evening Raider chose his campsite with extra care, doing his best to make it look as if he were being careless. He built up a big fire down in a little depression surrounded by heavy brush. He stuffed his bedroll with brush, to make it look as if someone were sleeping in it. He made sure that his horse was tethered tightly to a stout bush about twenty yards away.

As the fire died down, Raider stepped back into the brush. He figured the thick cover would embolden the Simes brothers. They would use it to get in close. The faint light of the fire would assure them that their intended victim was sound asleep, an easy kill.

When he was satisfied that he was well hidden, Raider made himself comfortable, waiting. An hour passed. He was wondering if they were going to come on in when he finally heard a rustling in the brush on the far side of the fire. He waited another five minutes. There. The outline of a man in the dark. Then another.

But where was the third? Raider didn't want to make his

move until he had all three of them out in the open. Too hard to locate the other one in the dark.

Raider had no choice but to wait. One of the two men standing at the edge of the brush raised his right hand. There was thunder and flame as his pistol roared. The muzzle flash was bright, almost blinding. Raider gritted his teeth as bullets thudded into his bedroll. The other man was firing now. Between them they fired more than half a dozen times, Raider's bedroll twitching under the impact of the bullets. Finally, the two men were satisfied and lowered their pistols.

One of them turned his head toward the brush behind him. "Jake, you can come on out now."

Smart. No wonder they'd remained alive so long. They had purposely left the third brother back in the brush to cover them while they did their murderous work. Raider saw the other man step out into the open, a rifle in his hands. The other two walked over to the bedroll. One of them kicked it with the toe of his boot. The bedroll skittered to one side, obviously far too light to contain a body. Instantly, the bandit stiffened. "What the hell...?" he burst out.

"Sorry you wasted all that lead, boys," Raider said quietly. The men all started to spin in his direction. Raider opened fire, aiming first at the man farthest away from him, an old trick so that his targets couldn't tell what was happening to their comrades. The man who had come out of the brush last flew backwards, crashing against a bush. Raider had time to fire again before the others returned fire. The man behind the one who'd kicked his bedroll went down, but not before getting off a shot. Raider rolled to the side as the third man opened up on him. Coming up onto one knee, Raider fired back, once, twice, putting both bullets into the man. He was the first to cry out, bellowing a hoarse grunt of pain as he staggered backwards. Raider shot him again and the man fell into the fire.

With only one round left in his pistol, Raider picked up his rifle. Normally he didn't like using a rifle at such close range, which was why he had begun the fight with his pistol. The first man he'd shot moaned, lurched to his feet, and staggered out of the bush into which he'd fallen. He had a pistol in his hand, so Raider shot him with the rifle. He fell back into the bush.

There was movement where the second man had fallen. A moment later light stabbed out from the dim form, accompanied by the crash of a heavy-caliber pistol. Lead lashed the air next to Raider's head, a damned good shot, but, as he'd done from the beginning of the fight, he'd been moving to the side, so the bullet missed.

Raider put two rifle bullets into the man and waited, but no shots came back. He could smell flesh and hair burning from the man who'd fallen into the fire, but he wasn't moving. Obviously dead.

He waited another ten minutes before leaving cover. Moving quickly, he knelt by the last man he'd shot. Dead, eyes open, staring sightlessly up at the moon. The one in the bush was still alive, but barely, apparently unable to move. Raider saw the man's eyes tracking him, but he could see no evidence of a gun on him, just the fallen rifle lying a few feet away. The man stared up at him. "You . . . you . . ."

A shudder, and he died. Raider kicked him hard with the point of his boot. No movement, just a loose rolling of the head. Raider made the rounds of each man, collecting their weapons, then he began collecting his own gear, cursing as he saw the holes in his bedroll. It took only a few minutes to saddle his horse and load his gear, then he mounted and rode off, traveling several hundred yards before dismounting once again and making another camp. He made no fire this time, merely unsaddled his horse and threw his bedroll down onto the ground. It was a warm night so he lay down on top of the bedroll, fully dressed, including his boots, and dozed until first light.

As the sky began to lighten, Raider once again saddled up, then cantered slowly over to the earlier campsite. It was not yet light enough for the buzzards to have begun work on the carcasses, but a few were beginning to circle high up in the sky. Raider heard growls as he approached

the campsite, and surprised several coyotes quarreling over
what was left of the Simes brothers. They were so fam-
ished, and so excited by such a magnificent windfall, that
Raider had to fire a couple of shots into the air with his
pistol to scare the animals away. Raider was sure he saw
one running off with a human hand in its mouth.

But the Simes brothers were not too badly chewed up.
Raider rode around the area in a big circle until he found
their horses, tied about a quarter mile away. They'd remained saddled and bridled all night. Since there had been
nothing to eat within reach of the ropes that pegged them in
place, they were glad to see Raider. He got down, untied
their lead ropes, remounted, and guided the animals back
to the campsite. They began to grow nervous as they
smelled the blood. Raider forced them on, lashing them
with a rope end. When he got back to the camp, one of the
coyotes had returned and was gnawing at the man who'd
fallen into the fire. Annoyed, Raider shot the animal,
which caused the horses he was leading to rear and bolt. It
was all he could do to hold them.

He finally managed to tie them to some of the heavier
bushes. Then he began loading the dead men. Now the
horses really began to spook, as the heavy, limp, bloody
bodies of their late masters were slung across their saddles
and lashed into place. But the lead ropes held, and within
half an hour Raider was leading the three horses, loaded
with the corpses, toward the nearest town, which, fortunately, was only a little more than thirty miles away, and
on his route anyhow.

He rode into the little town in the middle of the morning. It was the county seat, and there was a sheriff's office.
Naturally, riding into town with three dead men lashed to
their saddles attracted quite a bit of attention. Early
drinkers came out of the saloons, glasses still in their
hands. The lone barbershop emptied. Raider found the jail,
which was also the sheriff's office, with little trouble; it
was the only sturdy-looking building in town. The sheriff
had obviously been sleeping inside. He came out onto the
narrow boardwalk, blinking in the daylight, obviously only

half comprehending what he was seeing. Raider dismounted, looped his mount's reins over the hitching post, but tied the lead ropes of the other three horses securely. "Sheriff," he said. "We got us some business to discuss—inside."

"But . . . what the hell . . . ?" the sheriff burst out, staring at the three bodies.

"The Simes brothers," Raider said curtly.

The sheriff's mouth fell open. "Well, I'll be goddamned," he muttered, going over to inspect the men. Quite a crowd of flies had gathered, and the dead mens' faces were thick with them, especially around the eyes and mouth, where there was a little moisture. The sheriff waved his hands, scattering the flies, and bent down, studying all three faces, one by one. "Goddamn if you ain't right," he finally exclaimed, turning toward Raider. "But how—"

"Inside," Raider repeated, jerking his chin toward the jail.

The sheriff nodded, then led the way into the little building. It was fairly cool inside, since the walls were made of heavy adobe brick. The sheriff waved Raider to a chair and sat down himself in a big rocking chair next to a dilapidated desk. "What is it you got to say?" he asked, all business now.

"I work for the Pinkerton Agency," Raider said without preamble. "That buzzard bait out there tried to bushwhack me while I was sleepin'. They didn't do too good a job of it. Now, as you know, there's a reward of five hundred bucks a head on 'em, which, put all together, is a hell of a lot of money."

"Yep. That sure is one hell of a heap o' cash," the sheriff agreed, his little pig eyes lighting up at the thought.

"Uh-huh. An' normally, since I got 'em, the money should be mine."

"Yeah. But I hear Pinkertons ain't supposed to collect rewards," the sheriff replied, his eyes hooded.

"You're right. But there ain't nothin' about sheriffs not collectin' 'em, is there?"

"Uh-uh."

"So here's my proposition. We pretend you're the one who potted that coyote bait out there. You collect the reward—an' share it with me."

"Uh, what kind of cut would you be wantin'?" the sheriff asked cautiously.

Raider reflected a moment. Since he'd done all the really hard work, it wouldn't be out of line to demand at least two-thirds. But then, greed usually led to trouble, and the fairer he was now, the less hassle he might have with this thing in the future. "Fifty-fifty," he finally said.

The sheriff swallowed, shocked. "Seven hundred and fifty dollars!" he breathed out, indicating that he'd had at least a little arithmetic education sometime in the past. Raider could understand the man's shock. In a berg like this the local sheriff would be lucky to make fifty or sixty dollars a month. Raider was offering him a whole year's wages. "Jesus, I'll do it," the sheriff said.

Raider gave him the name of a bank he knew of in Kansas City, where he could send the money. The sheriff wrote it down, giving further proof of his scholarship. There was nothing to hold Raider here now. He turned to go. The sheriff stood up. Raider turned to face him again. "You'll make damned sure you send the money," he said, looking the other man straight in the eye. He saw, from the way the sheriff's eyes shifted away, that he might have been considering not doing it, but, pinned by Raider's remorseless gaze, the temptation quickly faded. "Sure. I'll send it," he promised.

Raider went outside, remounted, and within five minutes was out of town and heading east again across the prairie.

# CHAPTER ELEVEN

Three days later Raider was within a mile of Sarah's house. She lived in a remote area nearly ten miles from the nearest small settlement, and fifty miles from Kansas City. She'd homesteaded a quarter section, on which she ran horses and a few head of cattle. An old Mexican named Jesús was her only regular help. If she needed more help, at roundup time, or for breaking new colts, she hired it temporary.

Sarah was one of the most independent women Raider had ever met. Independent to the point of foolhardiness. It made him uneasy that she lived way out here on the edge of nowhere all by herself, with only old Jesús for company. Raider had said as much to her more than once, to which she always replied, "If you don't want me to be lonely, hang around a little more."

Which was an unusual thing for Sarah to say, to ask for male company. She was not a woman who trusted men. She had been married once, to a gambler, a good-looking, smooth-talking cardsharp who had on occasion run off with other women, usually coming back to Sarah, tail between his legs, when all his money was gone or someone was after him to collect a debt or to pay off an insult or injury. Finally, one night, his luck worse than usual, her husband had been in a game with three buffalo hunters. Out of money, but with a king-high full house, he'd put up his wife as his stake. Sarah was not presently in the saloon where they were playing, but the buffalo hunters had caught sight of her earlier in the day. "Done," one of the hunters had said. He was a huge man, awash in long stringy black hair, wearing filthy buckskins stiff from years of accumulated buffalo blood and grease.

Sarah's husband put down his full house, smiled, bent forward to rake in the pot. "Just hold on there a second, bub," the buffalo hunter said, fanning his cards out onto the table—a king-high straight flush. Sarah's husband stared at the cards for a few seconds, gave a sob of frustration and anger, because he really loved his wife, then reached for a small pistol he wore under his coat.

But the buffalo hunter was faster. He had a ten-inch skinning knife buried in the gambler's chest before his gun could clear leather.

Kicking the gambler's twitching body out of the way, the buffalo hunter stood up, collected his money, then signaled to his cronies. "Let's go pick up what we won," he grunted.

Raider found out what had happened a few hours later. He'd met Sarah a couple of times and had been impressed. In fact, he'd already fallen a little in love with her and wondered what the hell she was doing wasting her life with the weak, booze-ridden, gutless bastard she was married to. He'd actually asked her just that question once, and she'd admitted that she was beginning to wonder herself.

Not that Raider intended to offer her a solid alternative. He wasn't the kind of man who harbored thoughts of permanent relationships with women—although Sarah interested him more than most women. She was twenty-four when he first met her, an unusually beautiful young woman of medium size, with long dark hair and a lovely, intelligent face. And from what he could see, a fine body. But what interested him most was her apparent strength of character, her air of independence, the suggestion of intelligence and insight—not to mention the aura of intense sensuality that emanated from Sarah like heat waves.

Raider heard about the wager Sarah's husband had made about two hours after the buffalo hunters had carried her off. They'd been straightforward about it: they'd simply gone to the rooming house where she and her husband had been staying and informed Sarah that she now belonged to them. Sarah told them to go to hell and slammed the door in their faces. They immediately kicked it down and were on Sarah before she could get to a gun. They dragged her downstairs and threw her on a horse. Minutes later, the buffalo hunters and Sarah had disappeared out onto the prairie.

The moment Raider discovered what had happened, he collected his gear, headed for the livery stable, and saddled his horse. A few minutes later he was riding out of town, following their trail.

He had a good mount, and he could tell from the tracks that Sarah must be doing her best to slow down the hunters. He came in sight of them a little before dark, a group of four riders silhouetted against the sky about two miles ahead of him. He pressed on, closing the gap, but they'd seen him now, and a mile was as close as he could get. Being buffalo hunters, the men all carried big Sharps rifles. It was not unknown for buffalo hunters to pot buffaloes at over a thousand yards. A moving man on a horse made a more difficult target than a stationary buffalo, but not an impossible one. When Raider showed signs of meaning to follow them, a couple of the men dismounted. Raider whipped out his binoculars. The hunters were a long way off, but he could see them taking something from their packs, long sticks with a fork at the upper end.

Raider tucked the binoculars back in his saddlebags, turned his horse around, and began walking the animal away. Behind him, the hunters had shoved the sticks into the ground. They rested the long barrels of their rifles in the forked end of the stick, steadying them, flipped up the leaf sights to the correct range, which was about a thou-

sand yards, and settled in to aim. It was not easy to center
Raider in the sights; he was moving away at a slight angle,
but finally one of the men fired. A moment later the other
fired.

Looking back over his shoulder, Raider saw puffs of
white smoke balloon in front of the hunters. A second later
a huge fifty-caliber bullet whined by, plowing up dirt about
thirty yards past him. He kicked his horse into a canter,
zigzagging the animal back and forth, looking back to see
more white puffs of gunsmoke. He doubted the men could
hit him, but they might hit his horse, and then the chase
would be as good as over. Clapping spurs to his mount,
Raider put the animal into a dead run, still zigzagging. In
less than a minute he had ridden out of sight of the men
shooting at him.

Raider wondered if the buffalo hunters, knowing they
were being followed, would simply let the woman go. He
didn't really expect them to; buffalo hunters tended to be
hard, stubborn men. At least Raider now knew which way
the wind was blowing: he was going to have to fight to get
Sarah away from them.

It began to grow dark. Raider, trusting in the superiority
of his mount, rode far around to the left of the direction the
hunters had taken, in a big circle, with the intention of
getting ahead of them. He rode for three hours, pushing his
horse harder than he really wanted to, but unless he got to
the men in time, he doubted Sarah would be in any condition to even want to be rescued.

He almost rode too far. A little after two in the morning
he saw a campfire about two miles behind and to his right.
Turning his horse, he rode slowly toward it, doing his best
to keep to the lowest ground, searching out depressions
made by running water, so that he would not be silhouetted
against the sky. There was very little moon, which helped.
He halted his horse about a hundred yards away from the
campsite, intently studying the scene.

There were three horses standing hobbled near the fire.
And two men. And Sarah. She was standing crouched in
the firelight, half naked, her dress ripped from the neckline

down to the waist, facing two of the buffalo hunters. There was no sign of the third hunter or his horse.

Apparently Raider had made it in time; the hunters were only just starting to work on the girl. From the way she was standing, facing her captors, hands clenched, face taut, it still looked like she had plenty of fight left in her. Raider wondered why she didn't run away into the darkness until he noticed that she had a rope tied around her right ankle. One of the hunters was holding the other end of the rope, and he now pulled. Sarah's right leg flew out from beneath her, and she fell hard on her back. The other man was on top of her immediately, trying to pin her down, but Sarah was fighting fiercely. Raider saw the man backhand her across the face. She lay still for a second, time enough for the second man to run in close and begin prying her legs apart while the other man moved in between her thighs, fumbling with his pants.

Raider was tempted to move in at once, but he was worried about the third man. If the missing hunter was standing just out of the firelight with his rifle, riding in now would get Raider nothing but a bullet. Then, a break. He saw something moving out in the brush on the far side of the fire. A moment later a horse and rider appeared, the third man, holding his big Sharps in his right hand, the butt balanced on his right thigh. "Goddamn it!" he sang out. "You boys are tryin' ta hog it all while I freeze my ass off in the weeds."

The man who'd crawled between Sarah's thighs immediately leaped up. "Get the fuck back on guard!" he shouted to the horseman. "That son of a bitch who was followin' us could be back out there anywhere, sneakin' up on us right now."

Which he was, but coming in from the opposite direction. Raider moved his horse in slowly, wanting to get as close as possible before they discovered him. Fortunately, Sarah was attracting most of their attention. As soon as the men had started to argue, she'd made a break for the brush. The man with the rope tripped her again and started to haul her back, while the man who'd been shouting at the horseman scrambled after her. The mounted man was guffawing loudly.

Thirty yards away from the fire, Raider suddenly spurred his horse and raced toward Sarah and the men. They heard the hoofbeats, but by then it was too late. Raider's horse loomed out of the dark, Raider low in the saddle, the big Remington pistol in his hand. He shot the man with the rope first. The other man, the one on top of Sarah, leaped to his feet, pistol in hand, but his pants were unfastened and Sarah jerked on one pant leg, upsetting the man's balance. By then, Raider had ridden up right next to him and shot him in the chest. He wheeled his horse abruptly, which saved his life, since the mounted man had his Sharps to his shoulder by now and was pressing the trigger. But in close action the length of a rifle barrel, particularly a long-barreled rifle like the man's big buffalo gun, can be a handicap. The bullet ripped through the air an inch or two from Raider, scorching flesh.

The Sharps is a single-shot breechloader. The buffalo hunter levered the breech open, ejected the spent shell casing, then tried to ram another one in; but Raider was riding straight at him now, so the man dropped the rifle and groped for his pistol. Raider shot him before he could fire, but the hunter was a big, hard man, and he refused to fall. Grimacing, he thumbed back the hammer on his pistol, so Raider shot him again, knocking him half over the rear of his horse.

But still he wouldn't fall, or let go of his pistol. Raider had to shoot him twice more before he finally hit the ground.

Which had all taken time. Raider spun his mount, aware that his pistol must be empty by now. One of the bandits, the one with his pants down around his ankles, was crawling toward the pistol he'd dropped when Raider first shot him. Raider spurred his horse forward, dropping his pistol and jerking at the butt of his rifle, knowing that the man would reach his pistol first—if it had not been for Sarah. With a low cry of anger and hatred, she leaped forward, slamming into the man's back. They went down, the two of them, Sarah with her legs wrapped around the man's body. Raider had his rifle out now, but couldn't shoot without a good chance of hitting Sarah.

He didn't need to shoot. Sarah, still on the man's back, had managed to pull his skinning knife from the sheath at the back of his belt. She didn't know it, but it was the same knife that had killed her husband. Raider saw the bright gleam of the blade in the firelight as it rose high, then sliced down, tearing into the man's chest. He screamed, dropped his pistol, fought to turn and shake the woman from his back, but Sarah hung on, the knife rising and falling, and by now the red on it was not caused by the glow of the fire. She must have stabbed the man a dozen times before Raider dismounted and took hold of her hand. The man lay under her, eyes glazing, a horrified look on his face, the last of his breath whistling out of his gaping mouth.

Sarah, feeling the hand on her wrist, turned on Raider, a snarl on her face, and for a moment he thought he was going to have to fight her. Then she finally recognized him, and the light of battle slowly faded from her eyes. "Oh God. I'm so glad you're here," she half whispered.

She had begun to tremble. Raider held her in his arms, very aware of the ruined state of her clothes, of her bare breasts pressing against him. She began to shudder, and he thought she must be crying, but the girl was only trying to get herself under control. When she looked up there were two single tear tracks coursing downward through the dirt on her face, but that was all. She was covered with blood, but after making a quick examination, Raider came to the conclusion that very little, if any of it, was hers.

Sarah looked around the little camp, at the sprawled bodies. Then she looked back at Raider, trying for a moment to pull up the front of her dress to cover her breasts, then gave it up. She looked him straight in the eye. "I want to get out of here. Now."

Raider walked over to where the buffalo hunters' horses were tethered. He took the best one for her, then unsaddled the others and whipped them away into the night. He tried to offer her one of the blankets the buffalo hunters had spread out on the ground, but it was filthy and full of lice, and she waved it away, so in the end he draped his slicker over her shoulders, helped her to mount, and they rode away into the night, leaving the buffalo hunters for the coyotes and buzzards.

He took her only a few miles, to the bank of a small stream he had passed earlier. He dismounted, unsaddled the horses, and began to make a fire, while Sarah disappeared into the dark in the direction of the stream. He could hear splashing. A few minutes later Sarah returned, with his slicker still around her shoulders, but clean now of the blood that had covered her.

The girl stared into the fire while Raider opened a can of hash and heated it over the coals. She refused to eat until he had eaten a little, and then she wolfed the rest down. "I'm tired," she said when she had finished eating. "I want so very much to sleep."

It was nearly dawn by now, and fairly cold. Raider spread out his bedroll near the fire. It was a good bedroll, one he'd made out of an old overcoat and some quilts, all sewn together to make a nice pouch to slide down into, and covered with oilskin in case of rain. He hoped the girl would not reject it. He'd cleaned it a few days before, staking the roll down next to an anthill for two days so that the ants would invade the bedroll and eat anything living inside, an old Indian trick. He turned away as the girl pulled off the ruins of her tattered and bloody clothing and slid naked into the roll. Raider went over to lie on the hard cold ground, on the far side of the fire, partially covered by his saddle blanket. He'd been lying there for about ten minutes when the girl spoke. "They told me they killed my husband," she said. "Is that true?"

Raider hesitated. "I'm afraid it is," he finally replied.

"Oh," was all she said, her voice quite small.

Another few minutes of silence followed, then she spoke again. "I'm cold . . . I'm scared . . . I'm lonely. I want you to get in here with me."

Raider hesitated again. "Please," she said, her voice almost inaudible. That was the first and last time in their relationship that Raider ever heard her sound so lost. He got up, walked over to the bedroll, sat down, pulled off his boots, set his gunbelt down next to the bedroll, and gingerly slid inside, feeling her making room for him.

"Your belt buckle is hurting my skin," she said.

Raider pondered that one for a moment, then got out of the bedroll and stripped off his clothes. All of them. This time, when he slipped back into the bedroll, he was intensely aware of the heat of her bare skin, sliding by his. She moved against him. Her face was only inches away from his own. He could see her eyes, open, examining his face. Her arms circled around him, drawing him close, her legs opening so that his knee ended up between her thighs. "Well, I'll be goddamned," he muttered, his hand tentatively moving over her breasts, aware of the hardness of the nipples and of the rapid panting of her breath against his ear.

Her lovemaking was wild, almost savage. Raider had seen it happen before with other women, when, after sudden danger, and in the presence of death, an overwhelming urge to make love, to reassure life, swept over them. This was as intense a reaction as any he'd seen. He and the girl made love again and again, until finally, with a satisfied little sound coming from way back in her throat, Sarah fell asleep.

They patched up her dress the next morning, so that she was mostly covered again, and then they headed back toward town. She was full of light and life that day, casting warm glances in Raider's direction, and full of talk, too, explaining about her husband, how she had married him when she was very young, charmed by his good looks and glib tongue. She was from a fairly well-to-do family, a family that stifled her with its stodginess, until one day her Bible-thumping father, after months of looking at her ripe young body, had made a grab for her, which the nimbler girl had managed to avoid. But from then on she knew her days at home were numbered. Which suited her well enough, so that when her husband-to-be came along, she was ready to ride.

In her innocence she'd insisted on marriage, which she'd later come to regret. The fact that they were married made a difference to her, probably a residue from her up-bringing. Whatever the provocation, she had not found it easy to leave the man, even after she had, all too soon, discovered his general worthlessness.

By the time they got back to town Raider felt he'd known Sarah forever. Talk was easy between them, something new to Raider, who had never felt at ease in conversation. He didn't fully realize it, but he had been growing increasingly lonely. For years he'd had a partner, Doc Weatherbee, a man very unlike Raider, from an eastern background, well-educated, well-dressed, full of big words, a man Raider had often thought he could not stand —until the little bastard had finally gone off and married a rich girl. Now Raider's trails and campsites were solitary ones.

Once they were back in town Raider stared down any bothersome questions from the locals, while Sarah went up to her room and changed into another dress. Her husband had already been laid out by the local undertaker, who was now overjoyed at the prospect of actually being paid for planting the latest saloon casualty. The funeral was per-formed the afternoon they got back. Sarah looked pensive, standing by the graveside, perhaps even sad. Raider said nothing, but after the brief funeral the girl packed her few belongings and got ready to leave town. Raider met her outside her room. "Are you going on back home?" he asked.

"I don't have a home. Not yet," she replied.

"You gonna look for one?"

"Maybe."

She looked up at him. "Are you going to help me find one."

"Maybe," he said. And they'd ridden out of town to-gether, heading east.

# CHAPTER TWELVE

Now, more than a year later, Raider was once again riding up to the place where Sarah had decided to settle. She'd insisted that she wanted to be out on her own, away from other people—except for Raider himself, of course. He was gone most of the time anyhow, off wherever his work took him. Raider had been concerned about it, a woman in this rough land living away from the protection a town might afford, but he didn't complain too strenuously, suspecting that Sarah's current desire for solitude might be her way of dealing with her experience with the buffalo hunters. So he left her there with Jesús, alone for months at a time. Not that their relationship was any less intense when they were together. Raider had ample evidence that Sarah's passion for him was as great as his own for her. At first he'd been uneasy, waiting for her to demand that he leave his work and remain with her, as women tended to do. But she had not. Quite the opposite. When he'd finally brought it up himself, she'd emphatically said no, that Raider was not the kind of man to settle down, that he'd go crazy trying to live a sedentary life. He was grateful for her understanding. Not that it was easy, being away from her so much, but his homecomings were all that much the sweeter.

The dogs saw him first. Their barking alerted old Jesús, who came running up onto the porch to stare in his direction, crinkling up his dimming eyes. Finally, sure that it was Raider, he ran to the front door and shouted inside that the man himself, the hombre, had come home once again.

By the time Raider was at the hitching rail, swinging down off his horse, Sarah had come out onto the porch too. He saw that she must have been working with the colts again, because she was wearing a pair of men's dungarees, which were stiff with horse sweat. "Raider!" she cried out in that wonderfully uninhibited way she had. A moment later she had leaped off the porch and thrown herself into his arms.

Jesús discreetly made himself scarce for the next couple of hours, while Raider and Sarah renewed their acquaintance. It was a passionate two hours, beginning with that first embrace next to the porch and ending in the big double bed Sarah had had lugged all the way from Kansas City. Finally, with both of them naked, spent, and sated, it was time for conversation.

"Where've you been?" Sarah demanded.

"Wyoming, mostly. Up around Jackson Hole, then down to Cheyenne."

"Mmmm . . . you don't sound too happy with whatever it was you were doing."

"Nope. Dirty work. A man oughtn't to have to do some of the things I've been doing."

"Then stop doing them."

Raider looked over at Sarah. How beautiful she looked, with her face flushed from their lovemaking, dark damp tendrils of hair sticking to her neck and shoulders. Her body was a little leaner than when he'd first met her; breaking colts would do that to a person, but there was still one hell of a lot of woman there. And how like her, that response—if you don't like it, drop it. "Well, yeah . . . maybe," he finally replied.

And the idea began to grow inside him. "Yeah...
maybe," he repeated, staring off into space.

"Maybe what?" she demanded, poking him playfully.

He turned to her then, his face animated. "Let's get the
hell out of here. Just take off, the two of us. Go on out to
California. I've been there before, and I liked it, at least to
take a look at. We could go on up to San Francisco. That
was maybe Doc's favorite town, you know. Then when it
starts to get a little colder, we could go on down to the
southern part, around Santa Barbara and Los Angeles.
Ain't much there, really, but it sure as hell is nice and
warm in the wintertime. They grow oranges there. We
could pick 'em off the trees. Spend a few months just
doing whatever the hell we want to do."

Sarah laughed. "You're talking like a rich man."

"Well, I am rich, kind of."

He told her about the Simes brothers, and the reward
that should be coming into the bank in Kansas City. That,
plus the three hundred dollars he already had, plus whatever Sarah had, plus his back pay, should see them through
some good times.

He expected Sarah to start poking fun at his penchant
for wandering, but she didn't. Sarah had begun to grow a
bit tired of all this nest-building; breaking horses was becoming more chore than fun. Her memories of the buffalo
hunters had faded almost to invisibility. "I think we could
do it," she said eagerly. "Jesús has some family coming up
from Mexico, two sons with their families. They could run
the place while we're gone; they need the work, so I'm
sure they'd jump at the chance. And Jesús needs more help
anyhow—he's getting awfully old. Oh, let's do it,
Raider!"

"Done."

The next few days were given over to enthusiastic planning. They would ride the train all the way out to California, then, once there, do most of their traveling on
horseback. Raider felt fortunate in having a woman who
liked to travel the way he traveled, hard traveling, but
close to the earth, traveling where you had a chance to see

the ground you were moving over. He was immensely pleased at the thought of having Sarah riding next to him. Their money would run out eventually, of course. Raider wondered what kind of work he could take up that would allow him to remain close to Sarah.

Jesús's sons and their families were due to arrive by the end of the month. At the beginning of the last week of the month, Raider set out for Kansas City, to see if the reward money had come into the bank. If it hadn't, he would simply ride west and convince the sheriff to give him his share.

Raider rode easy along the way, taking his time, not arriving in Kansas City until the evening of the second day. He took a room in a small hotel, and was at the bank first thing in the morning. The money had arrived. Raider asked for it in banknotes and gold coin. The bank also handled Sarah's account, and Sarah had given Raider a draft to cash for her. The bank manager knew them both. He was a chatty man, and was soon doing his best to involve Raider in a conversation, to which Raider replied absently, until his attention suddenly snagged on something the bank manager had just said. "What's that? Some men were asking for me?"

"Uh-huh. Three of them. They said they were good friends of yours, that they'd met you in your . . . work."

Raider could think of no friends of his who knew that he had an account in this bank. "Who were these men?" he demanded. "What did they look like?"

"Well, actually," the bank manager said, a little alarmed at the vehemence of Raider's reaction, "they were a strangely mixed bunch. One of them—he seemed to be the dominant one—was a most cultured man, an intriguing conversationalist. We had quite a talk about banking practices, a most knowledgeable individual. The other two, however, were cut from much rougher cloth. I assumed they worked for him."

"Their names. I'd like to know what names they were using."

"Why, I . . . I don't know if they actually gave me their names."

"Never mind. Just tell me where they went."

"Well, come to think of it, I'm a little surprised that they haven't found you already. I gave them pretty clear directions. They should have run across you on the trail, unless you passed each other at night."

"Directions? Directions to where?" Raider demanded sharply.

The manager was quite shaken now. "Why, to Miss Sarah's place. I knew that if you were in the area, you'd be—"

"Ah, you goddamned fool," Raider snarled. Before the shocked manager could shut his gaping mouth, Raider was out the bank and heading for the stables where he'd lodged his mount. Five minutes later he was riding out of town like a madman, driving the animal mercilessly, wondering if he would be in time. The bank manager's description of the three men could easily fit John Van de Witt, Breaker Jackson, and Ernie Duval. The thought of them heading for Sarah's place was already making Raider sick to his stomach.

Later that afternoon he had to slow his pace; his horse was beginning to falter. He rested the animal the shortest possible time, then pressed on. By the time he reached the house, the animal was ruined, only a few miles away from dropping dead. Raider dismounted two hundred yards short of the house, concealed in a small stand of trees. Leaving the dying animal blowing its last in the trees, Raider continued on foot, moving fast but quietly, his .44 in his hand, his heart pounding. God, let it be all right! Let them not have come here!

But it was not all right. He found old Jesús lying half underneath the porch, shot twice through the chest. An ancient cap-and-ball Colt trailed from the old man's dead hand. He'd tried to make a fight of it.

Abandoning caution, Raider ran through the house. He

found only empty rooms, a deserted building devoid of life. Sarah was nowhere to be found.

He had not noticed the note the first time he'd passed through the living room. Now, coming downstairs, he saw it lying on a low table next to Sarah's big couch, the one she was so proud of. Raider scooped up the note, his eyes flying over it once, then returning to the beginning to take in the words more slowly. The note read:

"Raider. Sorry we missed you. We do not, however, consider the trip totally wasted, being grateful for the opportunity of meeting the charming young woman who lives here. I suspect that she is someone who means a lot to you. How fitting. I understand that you yourself had the good fortune to spend some time with my wife and children. I would now like to repay you for your kindness. We have taken the girl with us. Follow along, if you like. We'll do our best to leave bits and pieces of her along the trail."

The letter was signed, "John Van de Witt." As if Raider had not already known.

The trail, the trail, the letter had mentioned the trail. He had to get on their trail. He raced for the corrals. Van de Witt and the others had taken most of the better stock, but there was one animal remaining that looked as if it would carry him. He had it saddled and bridled within a few minutes, then raced out of the yard without looking back.

As he rode, Raider could not get Van de Witt's words out of his mind: bits and pieces of Sarah, along the trail. He had to look at the ground to follow their spoor, and he kept expecting to see things he did not want to see, bits and ieces. There were none, however, other than one of Sarah's scarves, which he found hanging from a bush where the trail forked, as if either she, or maybe Van de Witt, had placed it there so that he would be sure to notice where they had left the main trail.

His horse gave out around the middle of the night. Hearing a dog barking in the distance, he guided the stumbling animal toward an isolated farmhouse. The farmer nearly shot him when he began pounding on the door, but was glad enough to sell him a horse for the exchange of his own, plus fifty dollars.

It was a sorry nag, and was beginning to play out on Raider when, just after dawn, he came in sight of an old house situated on the side of a hill about a mile away. He had been pushing along the trail in the dark, gambling that his quarry would keep heading straight, and now that it was light he saw that they had. Their tracks led straight toward the house.

Raider rode in slowly. The place looked deserted—there were no horses tied up outside, no signs of occupancy. He almost rode on, convinced they had merely rested here before continuing on their way. Then he suddenly noticed something moving near one of the windows. Raider jerked his horse to one side, reaching for his Remington; then he saw that it was only a piece of cloth, hanging half out of the window and fluttering in the morning breeze.

It took him a second to recognize the piece of cloth as part of a dress he'd seen Sarah wear many times. The one she wore when she had chores to do that did not include forking a horse.

Raider threw himself off his mount and ran into the house. His eyes went to the piece of cloth. It was by itself, draped over the windowsill. He continued to search the house, always moving, so that he would be a difficult target. It was when he passed by a door leading into another room that he finally saw Sarah.

She was laying, naked, on a dirty mattress that had been thrown down onto the floor. The amount of blood told him, even before he reached her, that she must be dead. Still, he could hope, and kneeling next to the mattress, he looked into her staring eyes, calling out softly, "Sarah?"

No answer but the voice of the dead, the buzzing of flies gathered around the congealed blood. Raider placed a hand on her arm, shuddered at the icy, clammy deadness of the flesh, the obscenity of it, and then he leaped to his feet and began running through the house, screaming, "Van de

Witt! Come on out, you bastard. Come on out and I'll blow your guts all over the walls!"

There was no answer, only silence. Raider ran outside, searched the brush near the house. Nothing. Only tracks, leading away into the distance.

It was very difficult for Raider to go back into the house. Finally, he forced himself to walk into the room with the mattress, avoiding looking at what was left of Sarah. A minute or two passed before he saw the note poking halfway out from beneath the mattress. He bent, picked it up. "Pinkerton man," it said. "Once again we'd like to thank you for your kindness in permitting us to get to know your intended. As it turned out, we got to know her very well, before she finally decided to leave us. I thank you, Jackson thanks you, Duval thanks you. And I also thank you on behalf of my wife."

The note had been meant to wound, to tear, and it did. The words ripped into Raider as he glanced from the note down to Sarah's butchered body. But Van de Witt's words did something more. They engendered in Raider a violent desire for revenge, a white-hot need to kill. "You're a dead man, Van de Witt," he murmured softly. "You too, Jackson. And Duval. Every mother's son of you is gonna die. And you're gonna die hard."

# CHAPTER THIRTEEN

What little was left of Sarah's clothes was too torn to put
back on her body, so Raider wrapped her in an old blanket
he found in another room. Her body was limp and heavy
when he picked it up, and the head rolled loosely. Careful
not to look down at his burden, Raider carried Sarah out of
the house. His horse tried to shy when Raider slung the
bloody corpse over the saddle, but the animal was far too
tired to object strenuously.

Once Raider had Sarah lashed into place, he looked
down the trail in the direction Van de Witt and the others
had ridden. He could see the marks of their horses' hooves.
It was difficult to stifle the urge to follow, but he knew that
his horse was far too played out to go very far at a fast
enough pace to make pursuit worthwhile.

And, of course, there was Sarah. He knew she would
want to go back home, to the place where she had felt safe.
Strange. He had rescued her once from just such an ending
as this. That had been their bond. Raider was no philoso-
pher, but he couldn't help thinking that perhaps this was

the way she had been fated to die. His earlier intervention had only delayed the inevitable, not stopped it.

Raider began to walk back the way he had come, leading the horse; there was no chance of the exhausted animal carrying both of them. He had only walked about a mile when his feet began to hurt. His boots, with their high heels and pointed toes, were definitely not designed for walking. Like most horsemen, Raider only walked when there was no alternative, even if the distance to be traveled was less than a hundred yards. But the nature of Raider's work had often, over the past years, caused him to do many uncharacteristic things, so he was prepared. He took a pair of moccasins from his saddlebags and exchanged them for the boots.

Even with the moccasins, walking was not easy. Sharp stones bruised his feet; muscles that were unaccustomed to this kind of exercise began to ache. He welcomed the pain, the humiliation of being on foot, because he knew he was guilty, at least partially, of Sarah's death. He'd been given so many chances to take out the boss and the others, but he had always held back, playing it safe, rationalizing his slowness to act. Now, with Sarah gone, he began to understand his uncharacteristic timidity. It had been Sarah herself, of course, or rather, their relationship, the importance of it, the unacceptability of not having it anymore, of dying and never seeing her again, that had made him hesitant to gamble on survival. Yes, it had paralyzed him, the fear of loss, that killer of freedom and spontaneity.

And in the end, his hesitation had killed Sarah. He had not taken out the killers, and they had been alive to . . .

Raider forced his mind off this particular channel of recrimination, replacing it with his sense of rage and loss, with his unbending intention of destroying the men who had killed Sarah.

He lost all track of time, stopping only long enough during the night to lie down on the ground and catch a couple of hours' sleep. Sometime after dawn he came in sight of the place where he had bought the horse that was now carrying Sarah. As he approached the house the farmer cast a worried look at the obvious corpse lashed to Raider's mount, but his concern changed to delight when Raider bought his own horse back for another fifty dollars, with an additional twenty thrown in for a battered old saddle.

Now that Raider was mounted again, he made much better time, arriving back at the house late that afternoon. He had expected to find Jesús's body half devoured by scavengers, but the body's position partially under the porch must have protected it, because, although Jesús was beginning to smell very bad, he was more or less in one piece.

Raider unlashed Sarah from the saddle and laid her on the porch. She was beginning to smell bad too, but Raider chose not to think about that. He unsaddled the horses and ran them into the corral. Then he went out to the barn to get a shovel. There was a little knoll about fifty yards from the house where Sarah had liked to sit and watch the sunsets. Raider made his way to the top of the knoll and began digging two graves. He had to finish the graves by lamplight, but eventually he had them dug, two deep dark pits in the ground. He laid the bodies in the graves immediately, but did nothing to cover them until daylight. He lay on the ground nearby, dozing from time to time, his .44 in his hand in case any scavengers came to molest the bodies.

The sunrise was very beautiful. Sarah had liked sunrises too. Just as the first warm rays began to touch the earth piled around the graves, Raider threw a handful of flowers into Sarah's grave, directly on top of her blanket-wrapped corpse. He had not had time to make coffins. He tossed the old cap-and-ball pistol in on top of Jesús. "You tried, old man," he murmured. "You did your best."

Raider stood for a long time, thinking, remembering, then he filled in the graves.

He spent another day nearby, resting. He didn't care to sleep in the house; there were too many reminders of Sarah inside. The next day he rode into the little town where Sarah had filed her land papers with the local lawyer. Raider knew that Sarah had family somewhere, and he thought she might want them to know. But after he had informed the shocked lawyer, an obvious alcoholic, reasonably sober at that early hour, the lawyer informed him that Sarah had recently had him draw up a will leaving the land and all she had to Raider. There was no mention of family.

Raider rode back to the house, feeling the weight of ownership heavy on his back. As he approached, he was surprised to see that there was someone at the house; people were moving near an old broken-down wagon that was parked by the porch. For a moment Raider could think only of the last visitors to pass by, Van de Witt and the others, and he spurred his horse into a run, his face twisted into a snarl.

But all he managed to do, as he galloped into the yard, pistol in hand, was scare the hell out of a family of Mexicans. A few questions established that Jesús's two sons had finally arrived with their families. All of them, even the little children, eyed Raider suspiciously. They had already noticed the graves and the abandoned look of the house, and they knew something was very wrong.

Raider explained to them that Jesús was dead. The women began to wail and tear their hair. The men took it a lot better. Their faces pinched inward a little, but their innate sense of dignity kept them from showing too much of their grief in front of a stranger. The men helped Raider make some grave markers. After they were in place, Jesús's people showed signs of being ready to move along. It was clear that they had no idea where they would go; they were obviously at the end of their resources. Raider saw that he would now have a way to cut loose the last of his belonging, the last of his ties to Sarah.

He insisted that the two men accompany him into town, where he deeded over the house and the quarter section to them. The men, stunned by this act of munificence, had the pride to object. "Don't get on your high horse," Raider cut in. "This land ain't comin' to you from me, or even from the señora who used to live here. It's comin' from your father, Jesús. He died defendin' it. In my book, that makes it as much his as anybody's."

Of course, once they finally decided to accept this thunderbolt from heaven, Jesús's family were overjoyed. A few hours earlier they had been destitute, nearly at the end of their rope. Now they were the owners of more land than they had ever before imagined owning. When Raider rode away the next day, their shouted blessings accompanied him for quite a ways down the trail.

Now, with nothing to weigh him down, with Sarah buried on her own land, with the land passed on, Raider was free to do what he had vowed to do as he had looked down at his lover's butchered body. Free to revenge himself on Sarah's murderers.

# CHAPTER FOURTEEN

Riding to the nearest railhead, Raider bought a train ticket for Chicago, where the Pinkerton National Detective Agency had its headquarters. He sold his mount before boarding the train; he would eventually need a better horse than the one he was currently riding. After checking his saddle, bridle, saddlebags, and rifle scabbard into the baggage car, he tucked his bedroll under one arm, picked up his Winchester, and boarded the second-class car.

Since the agency did so much work for the railroads, most of its operatives were routinely provided with free railway passes. These passes were usually only good for second class, which was fine with Raider. As he settled down onto the hard wooden bench, he grinned, remembering how his partner, Doc, used to use every trick in the book trying to upgrade the second-class passes to first class. The greedy little bugger had really loved luxury.

The routing was through Kansas City and St. Louis. As he changed trains in Kansas City, Raider thought about the bank manager who had so carelessly sent Van de Witt and the others toward Sarah. He loathed men who couldn't

keep their mouths shut. He also thought about the money
Sarah still had in the bank there. Under the terms of her
will, it was now his. There wasn't much, but he'd told
Sarah's lawyer to arrange to have it put into his name, not
that he had any personal desire for the money—there was
not that much of it anyhow—but if he needed additional
funds for expenses while he was on Van de Witt's trail, the
money would be there, on top of the nearly one thousand
dollars of his own he still had left.

He arrived in Chicago during the afternoon of the second day. Amazing things, trains, you could cover so much
ground so quickly. Of course, you couldn't look right down
at the ground and read sign, like you could riding a horse.
You couldn't dismount and feel soil under your feet. You
couldn't smell the earth and the grass and the trees; all you
could smell was soot and cinders from the engine. Fast,
though, when you were in a hurry. And Raider was in a
hurry.

After the train had chugged into the Chicago yards,
Raider picked up his saddle and checked it at the luggage
depot. He then headed for a hotel he knew of not far from
the station. He attracted a lot of attention as he walked
through the streets, a big man in trail-worn clothes, lugging
a bedroll and a big rifle, with a heavy revolver hanging at
his side. Twenty years earlier he would hardly have been
noticed at all, but Chicago—hell, even cities farther west
were getting so stuck-up civilized that any man who didn't
look like he belonged in a factory or office attracted attention.

One big beefy man, dressed in a shiny checked suit,
with a fuzzy vest stretched over his gut, and accompanied
by two young ladies, started to laugh as Raider walked
by—until Raider turned and looked him in the eye. The
laugh was wiped right off the big man's face. He carefully
nodded a polite greeting, then shooed the two young ladies
down the street ahead of him.

Raider had little use for cities. Sometimes they were
good for buying things you needed that you couldn't get
farther west, but that was about it. As he headed toward his

hotel, he felt hemmed in by the rows of buildings that rose several stories on either side of the narrow streets. He felt squeezed by the crowds of people jostling one another. Too damn many humans.

And the smell. Chicago was growing, and as its human population grew, so did its animal population, the tens of thousands of horses, mules, and other livestock serving the citizens. Their droppings and urine turned the streets into a stinking quagmire. Getting pushed off the boardwalk into all that muck was not a pleasant experience.

No one pushed Raider, and within twenty minutes of getting off the train he was checking into his hotel. It was a rather plain establishment, but adequately clean, and he knew no one would bother his gear. He spent another ten minutes washing off railroad soot, then he left the hotel and headed for the agency's offices. And a few minutes later, as he mounted the stairs to the office, he had every intention of calling in some old debts.

At first it looked like those debts were not going to be paid. "Raider," he was informed by Allan Pinkerton, "we're not too happy about our operatives running off on private vendettas. We know you've suffered a loss, but we also know that operatives who have too much of a personal interest in the cases they're working on tend to make a lot of mistakes."

"Then the hell with you. I'll go after 'em on my own," he said. He was heading toward the door when Pinkerton called out after him. "Hold on, Raider. Don't get on your high horse. I said we normally don't *like* to do it that way, not that we wouldn't. Seeing as you're the one who knows Van de Witt and the others by sight, your way is probably the only way we *can* do it. I just want you to think about what I said."

Raider promised that he would. He'd gotten what he wanted: the entire resources of the agency would now be behind him. Once they decided to take on a case, the Pinkertons backed their men to the hilt; they were remorseless. Anyone who harmed a Pinkerton operative was in for a world of grief.

Operatives. That's what old Allan had always demanded his men call themselves, not agents. The old man was a hard taskmaster. He insisted that his employees be not only the best technically, but the best in other ways, too. Operatives were expected to send in daily reports, not only for the information in the reports, but so that they would also learn regular habits. They were expected to lead moral lives—except for whatever sneakiness they had to engage in to net their prey, such as seducing a bandit's sister so that they could worm his whereabouts out of her. Moral turpitude in the service of justice was not seen by that tough old Scot as moral turpitude.

Raider spent the next couple of days going through the agency's enormous rogues gallery, thumbing through thousands of photographs, looking for likenesses of Breaker Jackson and Ernie Duval. Every time an operative collared a lawbreaker, dead or alive, he was expected to photograph the man, then send the photograph to the Chicago headquarters. The photographs were cross-indexed with the seemingly endless stream of reports coming in from operatives in the field, and from the agency's army of part-time, amateur informers. All over the nation, bartenders, sheriffs, bankers, herders, cowmen, saloon swampers sent in information, some doing it because they were thrilled to think of themselves as part of the Pinkerton Agency, some because they were looking ahead to the big rewards the agency paid.

There was already a wanted poster out on John Van de Witt, but Raider didn't find any photographs of Jackson or Duval. He did run across a small file on each man, detailing all that was known about him, his normal haunts, and a record of his crimes. Breaker Jackson had been out of his usual area of operations when Raider had met him. Usually, Jackson, no lover of cold weather, tended to roam the West Texas and New Mexico area. Duval, on the other hand, was right at home in the northern territories, and, several days later, after word had been telegraphed to informers all over that part of the nation, a report came back, telegraphed by a livery stable owner in Montana, that a man fitting Duval's description had passed through only the day before, heading farther west.

Raider was ready to ride within an hour. He checked back by the office before he left, to arrange lines of communication with his employers; they were always after Raider, who was not a man to spend time scratching on paper, to send in his reports more regularly.

"Remember," Allan Pinkerton said, "get permission for any expenses over fifty dollars."

Raider nodded. Damned skinflints. Fifty dollars didn't buy much anymore. He was glad he had his own money.

"And Raider," Pinkerton said as Raider started out the door. "Send us word if you get killed."

# CHAPTER FIFTEEN

Duval could hardly have picked a better place in which to hide. Montana was the last of the frontier, still quite sparsely settled and very hard to reach. Raider could not get there by what was usually the fastest way, by train, because the railroads had not as yet penetrated Montana. Oddly enough, the only established route was via steamboat, by the Missouri River from St. Louis, all the way across Missouri and part of Kansas, across Nebraska, South Dakota, North Dakota, and the entire width of Montana, to Fort Benton. The river trip, however, took weeks, and at this time of year, late summer, the rivers would probably be too low for river travel anyhow.

Retracing his journey, Raider took the train back to Cheyenne. From Cheyenne he would have to travel by horse, which meant that he first had to buy a horse. He spent two days in Cheyenne outfitting himself. Good horseflesh was not as plentiful as he had expected. He cursed himself for not buying a good mount in Chicago and having it shipped along with him on the train. He finally located a big bay that looked like it might have staying power, although it was a nasty-tempered animal, intolerant of being ridden. Or perhaps it was simply too intelligent to docilely allow human beings to sit on its back and order it around. Raider spent the better part of a day showing the horse who was boss.

He also purchased an extra horse, a lesser animal, to ride from time to time to rest his principal mount. The price for both animals was over a hundred dollars. This far out on the edge of the settled world, prices seemed god-damned high.

Raider made no attempt to contact the sheriff in Cheyenne. On the one hand he did not want to be reminded of Mrs. Van de Witt. On the other hand, he did not want to share information with anyone. Ernie Duval belonged to him, and to him alone.

There was little to slow Raider down during the first part of his journey—other than the harshness of the area he was passing through. The land was extremely dry this time of year, barren, hostile. He had to burden his horses with large amounts of water, not knowing the area well enough to be certain of finding water at the end of a day's ride. Or even at the end of two or three days.

Dust devils swirled around him, kicked into life by his horses' hooves. He changed mounts frequently, trying to save the animals while at the same time traveling as fast as possible. Four days out, he reached the north fork of the Platte River. It was a wide stream broken partway across by sandbars, yet swift enough even at this time of year to be dangerous. He turned west, riding along the south bank of the river for another day and a half before he found a place where it could be easily forded.

He headed north again. The land was less dry here. The next day he crossed the Powder River, and two days later, the Tongue. It was between the Powder and the Tongue that he had his first trouble with Indians.

Part of it was his fault: he had not expected to find hostiles this far south. The Army was keeping the Cheyenne, Blackfoot, and Crow busy in the northern part of Montana, or so he thought. The band he ran into was probably just a bunch of young bucks circling south for loot and glory. Riding over the top of a hill blind, without having scouted around to the sides, he nearly rode right into the midst of them. There were about a dozen, apparently Northern Cheyenne, all wearing war paint, most of them carrying guns.

Fortunately, the Indians were almost as surprised as Raider. Reacting immediately, he whirled his horses and raced away back the way he had come. A few seconds later the Indians were in full pursuit, yipping wildly, a few of them sending useless shots after him.

Fortunately the Indians were poorly mounted, and Raider quickly pulled away from them. The Indians, however, showed no signs of giving up the chase, which annoyed Raider. He was now heading in a direction in which he didn't want to go, and furthermore, he could see that his horses were tiring quickly. The Indians could see it too, and while their mounts were in even worse shape, Raider suspected that they would probably dog his trail until either accident or fatigue brought him to bay.

Raider rode on until he was out of sight of his pursuers. All the while he was studying the landscape around him. He finally found what he was looking for—a small hill that overlooked his back trail for a mile or so. He quickly dismounted, tied the reins of his second horse to his saddle horn, and looped the big bay's reins around his arm. Then he jerked out his Winchester and lay down on the ground, waiting.

A few minutes later the Indians came into view, strung out a little as weaker horses faltered, but there were eight of them out in front, fairly well bunched up. Raider raised the leaf sight at the rear of the Winchester and set the crossbar for the range, about six hundred yards. Then he set the set trigger; the slightest touch would fire the rifle. He sighted down the long barrel, holding his breath, watching his heartbeat, framing the leading warrior's mount in his sights, his finger pressing lightly against the trigger. The rifle seemed to go off on its own, slamming back against his shoulder, driving his body backward. The huge bullet was sent arcing out toward the Indians.

The lead rider's horse went down heavily, falling in full stride, throwing its rider over its head. The Indian lay in the dust, stunned, while his comrades raced by him.

And now the nature of Raider's Centennial Model Winchester came to his aid. Most big-bore rifles capable of packing so much wallop at such a distance, like the Sharps, were single-shot. Not the Centennial. Raider levered round after round into the chamber, firing rapidly. He missed some shots, but three more horses went down before the Indians wisely decided to ride back out of range. One lone warrior continued on toward Raider, either braver or stupider than the others, yipping wildly, a long lance clutched tightly in his right hand. There was no sign of firearm on him.

Raider admired the man's courage, but that was not what prompted him to aim for the brave's horse, rather than the brave himself. If he killed any of the Indians, the survivors would feel obliged to continue on after him, to avenge their fallen companions. As it was, they were losing valuable horses very quickly, with little to show for it but the probability of losing more.

Raider waited until the lone Cheyenne was within a hundred yards, then shot his horse out from beneath him. The rider, perhaps expecting this, did a neat somersault and landed well, staggering a few steps past his fallen, kicking mount. Then the man scooped up the spear he had dropped and came racing up on foot, still yipping wildly. Raider simply stood up, mounted, and cantered off, leaving the brave cursing and shouting behind him.

With a large number of their party now having to double up on the remaining horses, the Indians abandoned the pursuit. Raider rode around in a wide circle, heading back toward the south bank of the Tongue, but a bit more to the west than he'd intended.

The next day he crossed into Montana—with two very tired horses. The run from the Cheyenne, short as it was, had pushed the animals over the edge of exhaustion. They plodded on faithfully enough, but most of the fight had now been ridden out of the big bay. The second horse was limping slightly, still traveling, but far too slowly, and Raider knew that if he didn't rest both animals soon, they were going to end up useless.

He was now traveling through immense rolling grasslands. Montana grass was reputed to be of a surpassing richness, perfect for grazing animals. The buffalo had certainly thrived on it. Millions, tens of millions had formerly inhabited these plains, food for the Crow, the Cheyenne, the Sioux, the Flatheads, and many other tribes.

Then, back in the sixties, buffalo coats had come into fashion, both in the United States and in Europe. Soon, hide-hunters had entered the plains, slaughtering millions of the huge slow creatures for their hides only, leaving the carcasses to rot, strewing the horizon with countless whitening bones. Later, when buffalo coats went out of style, there was still no reprieve for the buffalo. The Army came into the area, with settlers not far behind, and the hunters continued the slaughter, this time for meat, to feed the Army, the railroad workers farther south, and the captive Indians penned up, starving, on barren reservations. Now the mighty buffalo herds were no more. The land Raider was passing through was nearly devoid of life, containing only a few antelope and some scrawny coyotes, all that man had left of the countless animals that had been thriving here only a decade earlier. But there was still all that grass, a perfect vacuum beckoning the cattleman.

The herds had begun to come in only a few years before, some driven all the way up from overgrazed Texas, others coming in from California and Oregon, where there were just plain too many cattle. Some even entered the plains from eastern Montana, where the herds brought in to feed the men who worked the mountain mines had overstepped the ability of that more rugged western land to feed them.

Raider ran into his first herd about a day's ride south of the Yellowstone. The first he saw of it was a huge cloud of dust maybe ten miles ahead. He pushed his horses on. An hour later he ran into the drag, three cowboys riding in the wake of the herd, making cetain that no animals fell behind and got lost. The riders didn't notice him until he was only a couple of hundred yards away, which was no surprise, since they were thickly covered with dust—their clothing, their faces, their horses white with it. The men all had bandannas tied around the lower part of their faces to keep as much of the dust as possible out of their noses and mouths. Riding drag was not looked on by the average cowboy as desirable work, but somebody had to do it, usually the men with the least seniority.

One man, his eyebrows dripping dust, finally noticed Raider. He quickly turned his horse and rode over to the drag rider nearest to him, about two hundred yards away. That rider, in turn, rode over to the next, while the first cantered toward Raider. Their caution suggested to Raider that they'd had troubles during the drive, which was not unusual in country as wild as the land they must have traveled through. Their gear established them as Texans. Montana was one hell of a long way from Texas.

"Howdy," the rider said to Raider. He was young, at the most in his early twenties, but looked whipcord tough.

"Howdy," Raider replied pleasantly. "The boss man around?"

"Up near the front o' the herd," the rider said laconically. "Reckon if you ride up that way, you'll find him comin' back."

Raider nodded, turned his mount, and headed into the dust cloud. He could see the individual cattle now, looming up out of the dust like small ships suddenly appearing in a dense sea fog. All of them were longhorns, none of those fancy new eastern breeds. It was a big herd, several thousand animals. Raider was about halfway up one side of the herd, the windward side, so that he was now out of the dust, when he saw three men cantering back toward him. The man riding out in front was big, and better-dressed than the others; he looked as prosperous as a man can look after riding for thousands of miles alongside a slow-moving herd of cattle.

The three men pulled their horses to a stop when they reached Raider. He noticed that they had partially fanned out around him. Cautious, all right.

"Silas Hornby's my name," the big man said. "What might you be doin' out this way?"

"Headin' for Helena, out west. Could use a little company right now. An' maybe a chance to buy another horse."

"Can't help you with the horse," Hornby said. "Our remuda is down too low right now as it is. As for the company, well, I expect most of the boys could stand looking at a new face by now. Ride on up with us toward the point."

They turned their mounts, leading the way toward the front of the herd. Raider's horses had trouble keeping up with the others. Hornby must have noticed, because once they had reached the dust-free point, out in front of the herd, he made Raider an offer. "Tell you what. You can turn your animals in with our remuda and borrow our nags for a couple of days. That way your animals will get some rest. You might have to work for it a little, though."

Raider gratefully accepted. One man was detailed to guide him back toward the remuda. Since all the work of driving cattle was done from horseback, which was hard on horseflesh, all trail outfits had remudas, herds of horses, so that the cowboys could change mounts, often several times a day, if the going got that hard.

When they reached the remuda, the man with Raider told the head wrangler, a young boy probably no older than sixteen, to let him cut out a mount. Most horse wranglers were young, usually too inexperienced for the intricate riding and roping work of a tested cowboy. Raider looped a noose over a fresh-looking animal, snubbed it to a bush, and transferred his saddle and gear from his tired mount. His horses were then chased in with the rest of the remuda. Even though the big bay was nearly worn out, he pranced in with the other horses head-up, looking around for the head stallion, ready for a challenge. The other horses snorted and shied at the intrusion, but horses being herd animals, Raider knew that his would be unlikely to run off, not as long as they had this much equine company.

Raider rode back up to the point, where he joined Hornby. Hornby nodded, but neither man said much for the first few minutes, until Hornby finally spoke up. "What might be takin' you out toward Helena. That's a fair piece down the road—if there was a road."

"I'm fixin' to meet a man thereabouts."

That was about as much as politeness permitted Hornby to ask—directly. He rode on a ways farther, ruminating. "You a lawman?" he finally asked.

"More or less."

Hornby took a long look at him. "Pinkerton?"

"Uh-huh."

Raider chanced a sidelong look at Hornby. He hoped the man would keep this latest information to himself. Cowboys, the working man in general, did not have much love for the Pinkerton Agency. They tied it in too much with the bosses—the rich—although there would probably be less of that with cowboys, since they were too free a breed to let bosses shove them around. Now, if they had been miners instead of cowboys . . . Miners had plenty of reason to hate the agency. Too many miners had been killed by Pinkertons when the miners tried to go out on strike. Raider tended to side with the miners. The Pinkerton men they hated came from another side of the agency, the protection side, the side that hired out guards and gunmen, men he had no use for.

Hornby seemed disposed to keep his peace. As they rode along, he began to loosen up a little. Clearly, he was tired of the trail and eager to talk. "We come up from down around San Antonio," he said. "Nearly five months nursemaiding these stupid lumps of meat." He swung his arm around in the general direction of the plodding cattle. "My range was about grazed out. Heard about the grass up this way from some others, who'd come up and liked it. So here I am, cattle, gear, men, and all. And I'll tell you—so far, I like the looks of this grass. The cattle are already startin' to put back on some of the weight they lost along the trail."

Raider chatted back for politeness; after all, he was riding the man's horse. His mind was locked onto Duval, however, still several days ride away to the west—if he was there at all, if Raider wasn't chasing down a false lead. But, despite his urge to ride west, he'd have to spend a couple of days with the herd, letting his horses get their strength back.

That night he had his first full meal in days, sitting around the fire with the hands, a big chipped enamel bowl of beef stew in front of him. The cowboys, particularly the younger ones, were a little shy around him; he was clearly of a different breed. The way he wore his .44, the gear he had, especially the look in his eyes, told them that he made his living in a much different way. But they were as friendly as puppies, and he felt himself warming to them. Theirs was a much less complicated life than his. No Ernie Duvals, no Breaker Jacksons. No Mrs. Van de Witts.

He went to sleep that night close to the fire. For the first time in a long time he didn't sleep with his horse's reins looped around his wrist. He didn't feel that he dared only doze, his senses alert for danger. The soft singing of the night herder, calculated to soothe the cattle, drifted in from the herd. Just before he finally went to sleep, he wondered what it would be like to live this kind of straightforward life, a life of freedom and hard honest work. A life spent on the back of a horse, each cowboy feeling that he was lord of creation, seated way up there so high, miles above the poor bastards working on, or under, the ground.

But even as he was thinking about it, he was aware that this kind of life could not survive much longer. He had seen the endless miles of fencing going up over thousands of square miles of what had once been open range. These same cowboys, if they remained cowboys, were eventually going to have to get down off their horses and dig holes for those fence posts. They were going to have to work at growing and harvesting winter fodder: once those fences went up, that would be the only way to feed confined herds.

But for the moment it was enough to lie by the fire, listening to the nighthawk's soft crooning and the good-natured joshing of the sleepy cowboys, to smell the ground beneath him, and for just a couple of days, not to have to be wary of the morning.

Raider stayed with Hornby's herd three days, until they reached the Yellowstone. Still mounted on Hornby horses, he helped move the herd across. The Yellowstone was broad and fairly deep. It was necessary to swim the animals across, both horses and cattle. Fortunately, the crossing went well, with only one or two cows lost. Hornby told Raider that they had been caught by floods down in Nebraska, after a storm, and had lost about three hundred head. And a man drowned when his horse rolled over on him crossing a river.

On the third day Raider left the herd, mounted once again on his own horse. The animals were in much better shape now, especially the bay. The other horse, the one he led most of the time, was strong enough for the moment, but he knew that it didn't have the bottom the bay had.

His route led due west, toward the western Montana mountains, the first part of the territory to be settled. Twenty years before, as the California gold fields began to play out, miners had pushed east, over the mountains, looking for more gold. They had found plenty of it in southwestern Montana. Towns like Bannack and Virginia City had sprung up, rough little towns, packed with miners desperate for gold, and with the parasites who preyed on those who worked—gamblers, whores, confidence men, bandits.

Raider had heard about those early days. There was, of course, no law in the area then, it was all too new. One particular band of outlaws, called, improbably, the Innocents, had terrorized the area, robbing and killing under the leadership of a man named Henry Plummer. Finally, the citizens had formed an efficient group of vigilantes. A large number of men had been hanged, including Plummer.

The area more or less settled down after that, but even now, due to the incredibly rugged nature of the land, western Montana was still a rough place. A natural bolt-hole for a man like Ernie Duval.

The farther west Raider traveled, the more difficult the land became, made up for the most part of rugged, very steep mountains, made to look spiny by tall thin conifers. In places the hills were denuded, where trees had been cut down to feed the hunger of the mines, the stamp mills, and the towns, for firewood.

The closer Raider got to the mining area, the more ravaged the land became, until finally, close to Helena, he was surrounded by a wasteland of gutted valleys and hillsides, where hydraulic hoses had washed away the soil in a frantic hunt for gold, where huge piles of mine tailings had been stacked up, after the guts had been ripped out of the interiors of mountains. He was nearing civilization again, the abode of men.

When Raider reached Helena, he first located the livery stable from which the wire had been sent concerning Ernie Duval. The stable's owner, the one who had sent the wire, seemed intelligent enough to have seen what he claimed to have seen, although there was still a chance he had been mistaken, that it was only someone who looked like Duval. But the stable owner was sure: he had reason to remember that particular man; he'd ruined a horse from the stable, then threatened to cut out the stable owner's guts when he'd protested. That certainly sounded like Duval.

The word was that Duval had been on his way toward Butte. There were gambling pickings there. Some maniacs were talking about developing the worthless copper deposits in a big copper mine down that way. The Anaconda mine. They were pouring millions into mills, roads, buildings, even planning to bring in the railroad. There was money there, a lure to men like Duval.

When Raider reached Butte, an ugly collection of shanty housing and mine pits, a little verbal digging in various saloons brought out the information that a man fitting Duval's description had been there and had gone on again, heading south, toward the old, played-out gold fields around Bannack, where Henry Plummer and his Innocents had earlier held sway.

Raider rode on, the land around him growing rougher and rougher. The area through which Raider was traveling showed little sign of human habitation, just scattered cabins here and there. For the most part he slept out on the trail, once again with the reins of the big bay looped around his wrist. It was the animal's nickering that woke him one night. Raider lay perfectly still when he awoke, listening, sniffing the breeze, trying to see in the dark. He knew something was wrong, but could not immediately tell what it was. It was fully fifteen minutes before he realized that his spare mount, which he'd hobbled some thirty yards away, where there was grass, was missing.

There was not much he could do until morning. As soon as it was light enough, he was on the trail, tracking the horse. Clearly someone was riding it. It was by far the weaker animal; recently it had begun limping again, so he knew he would have little trouble catching up to whoever had stolen it.

He came on the Indians about two hours after dawn. They were down in a little depression, six of them, all Flatheads—an old man, two scrawny little kids about eight years old, two youngish women, and an old crone so wrinkled and emaciated Raider wondered what was keeping her alive. All of them were wretchedly thin: they were clearly starving to death, which was why they had stolen the horse. The old man must have done it, a clever old warrior. With the buffalo gone, with their people imprisoned on reservations, starved by corrupt Indian agents who stole the tiny amounts of food the government allotted to the Indians, the old man, obviously the sole support of this little group, had had no choice but to go out and forage. Raider's mount had been near at hand.

The horse's throat had already been slit, and the women were cutting the animal up. A few strips of meat were already cooking over a small fire. Raider patiently sat his horse on the skyline; he did not see any indication of firearms among the people below. The old man saw him first. For a moment despair twisted the old warrior's features. Then he picked up a knife, and chanting, probably his death chant, started climbing up the side of the hill toward Raider.

Raider watched him come on. The old man knew he was going to die, but he was ready. Raider raised his hand in a sign of peace, but the old man continued to climb. He slipped once—he must have been very weak from hunger—and rolled partway back down the hill. Raider quickly dismounted and pulled some bacon and a couple of cans of beans out of his saddlebags, then tossed them down the hill. It was all the food he had. The cans rolled past the old man, who looked at them uncomprehendingly. Raider raised his hand again in the peace sign, then turned his horse and rode away.

He was not in a good mood when he reached the Bannack area. The old Indian's degradation had hurt him nearly as much as Sarah's death. He kept remembering the emaciated old woman, the starving kids.

On the way down he'd passed a few outlying homesteads. In such isolated areas, local gossip was a prime source of information for an operative. Out here, anything unusual was noticed, remembered, and passed on. And even in as rough an area as this, Ernie Duval was obviously such an evil little bastard that he would stand out clearly.

By the time Raider reached town, he knew he would find Duval there. He even knew in which saloon Duval tended to spend his time, what little of it he had left.

Time was about up for Ernie Duval.

# CHAPTER SIXTEEN

Duval spent most of his time in a seedy little saloon that matched the seedy little town in which he had holed up. Raider made no attempt to ride straight in and go for him. He didn't want it to end that quickly.

He made one nighttime pass through town on horseback, spying out the land, making sure he stayed in the shadows. Dim light flickered out through the saloon's half-open front door. He wondered if Duval was inside. Probably. But . . . all in good time.

He made camp about five miles away, in an area of dense brush where he knew he was unlikely to be seen. He didn't go back into town until the next night, covering the last couple of hundred yards on foot, leaving his horse tied to a tree beyond the farthest building. He moved close to one wall of the saloon. He could hear voices inside. The saloon had only one window, a grimy pane of glass located on a side wall. Raider positioned himself directly in front of the window and peered through it into the saloon.

The saloon was even seedier inside than outside. A scarred and sagging bar ran along one wall. Faded pictures hung crookedly, in great profusion. Old furniture littered the floor. There was little uncluttered space, what little there was being taken up by a huge, slightly swaybacked pool table. Two drunks were hunched over the ripped and stained green cloth cover, ineffectually poking bent pool cues at chipped balls. Ernie Duval stood on the opposite side of the room, leaning with his back against the bar, a glass of whiskey in one hand, lazily watching the two drunks' clumsy game of eight-ball.

Raider looked long and hard at Duval. The little bastard looked so much at ease! That had to be changed. Raider remained at the window, making no attempt to hide himself. A little light spilled out through the panes onto him, although the dirtiness of the glass probably made it difficult to see out very clearly. He would show up only as a shadowy image. He remained in place, willing Duval to look toward the window.

Eventually, Duval did. His eyes tracked over the glass lazily, swung on by, then jerked back again. He stared for several seconds, his entire body tensing, then he turned and ran toward the door.

By then Raider was already gone. He simply melted back into the darkness, moving into the cover of some trees just a second or two before Duval came striding quickly around the corner of the building. The darkness stopped him. He hesitated, staring into the night. "Who the hell's out there?" he demanded.

Raider remained perfectly still. He doubted Duval would come toward him to investigate. Walking from the light into darkness, toward a potential enemy, was too foolhardy an act, even for a nut like Duval.

As if realizing his vulnerability, Duval walked back around the corner. A moment later Raider heard the rusty hinges of the saloon door squeal. Apparently Duval had gone back inside, but Raider continued to remain motionless for another few minutes. Sure enough, after a short wait, Duval's head slowly appeared around the corner of the building, peering into the dark. He had only pretended to go inside.

He held his position for several minutes, then finally shrugged, turned around, and disappeared from view. This time, when the door hinges squealed, Raider was certain Duval had gone back into the saloon.

Raider quietly moved away, toward his horse. Chances were that Duval would begin to believe that it had been only his imagination, creating ghost images in empty windows. Duval would be a man who knew about ghosts.

Raider lay low for another day. By now he had discovered where Duval was sleeping—in a small cabin about a quarter of a mile outside town. Raider visited it one afternoon while Ernie was in the saloon. There was no lock on the door, so slipping inside was easy. The interior of the cabin turned out to be pretty shabby diggings for a man who'd ridden with one of the most successful gangs of robbers in the West, but then, Duval had never shown much aptitude for hanging on to money. The single room was small and poorly furnished, if it could be called furnished at all, with a narrow broken-down bed in one corner, a chipped washbasin that looked like it had seen little recent use, and a three-legged stool lying on its side near the bed.

Raider had brought a bundle with him, and now he opened it. Unfolding a large piece of cloth, he laid it full-length on the bed. Even in the dim light inside the room the bloodstains on the ripped and shredded cloth showed clearly, in huge brownish patterns. It was what had been left of Sarah's dress.

He was watching from a distance through his binoculars when Duval went into the cabin. For several seconds nothing happened, then he heard a cry from inside, and a moment later Duval came running out the door, holding the torn dress in one hand, his pistol in the other, looking around wildly. Seeing nothing, he threw the dress down onto the ground. "What the hell is going on?" he shouted. His pistol barrel tracked first in one direction, then in another. "Godddamn it!" he screamed. "If you're there, come on out into the open and face me man to man!"

Nothing answered him but silence. Duval, perhaps feeling vulnerable with all that empty land around him, ducked back inside. Raider slipped away quietly. He wondered how long Duval would stay in the cabin, trying to puzzle out what was happening to him.

He would, no doubt, suspect that Raider was somewhere nearby. Who else would have had access to that dress? As days passed and Raider failed to appear, maybe the little bastard would begin to wonder if his mind was playing tricks on him, if maybe Sarah had come back from the grave. He was loco enough.

But Ernie Duval's particular brand of insanity was not the kind that could be fazed by guilt; he had no conscience at all. The next time Raider caught sight of him he was walking about as if nothing at all had happened.

Time for more direct action. The next morning Raider posted himself on a ridge overlooking Duval's cabin. Since Duval usually came in from the saloon quite late, he was not an early riser. Raider waited until noon, then thought he saw signs of life from inside the cabin. About ten minutes later Duval came outside, shirtless and without his boots, heading for the outhouse. Raider let him get within about ten yards of it, then opened fire with his Winchester, not trying to hit, but shooting close.

The heavy bullets kicked up big clouds of dirt around Duval. He froze for a second, hunching up his shoulders; clearly he was only half awake, but he now came awake very quickly and sprinted for the cover of the house. Raider kept on shooting, the bullets kicking up dust only inches behind Duval's bare feet. Duval dived in through the door, obviously heading for the floor.

Raider kept shooting, blowing out the single window, shredding the door, wrecking the rickety stovepipe. Finally satisfied, he walked down the back side of the ridge toward his horse. As he rode away he could hear the light pop of Duval's pistol, mixed with hoarse curses. He wondered what Duval was shooting at. More ghosts? Smiling grimly, Raider imagined Duval trying to dig his way down through the splintery floor while those big .45-caliber bullets wrecked the cabin around him. He hoped the little bastard had shit his pants.

Duval left town later that day. It was a hasty departure. Raider sat his horse, concealed near the crest of a hill, watching Duval whip his mount out onto the trail. Raider waited a while, rode into town, bought some supplies, then set out on the same trail.

For the first few miles Duval's sign was easy to follow; he was making no attempt to hide his tracks. Raider rode on leisurely until instinct and training told him it was time to start taking Duval a little more seriously. Swinging off the main trail, he headed for higher ground. Two hours later he spotted Duval's ambush. Ernie had hidden himself on a small rise overlooking his back trail. Raider could see the muzzle of a rifle poking out of a clump of brush. Raider positioned himself behind some trees and repeated his earlier performance, raining bullets around Duval. Given the much greater range of Raider's rifle, Duval had no choice but to run for it and hightail his way down the trail.

Raider ran Duval for three more days, driving him to the edge of madness. He was now letting Duval see him, showing up for a few seconds on the skyline, perhaps only two or three hundred yards away, then disappearing before Duval had a chance for a shot. Duval did not have the trailcraft to really come after him. He was a barroom animal; he relied on his own viciousness to cow others. Out here, in the wilderness, his viciousness gained him nothing.

Raider ran him due south into some of the roughest country he'd ever seen. It was all mountains, hard mountains, shaley, steep, with crumbling slopes, sparsely wooded with the same spiny conifers as farther north. Water was scarce, and Raider suspected that Duval, who was not good at finding water, was becoming thirsty.

And increasingly desperate. Hidden half a mile away, Raider watched Duval leading his horse onto hard ground, obviously trying to conceal his trail. Raider let him think he had succeeded. For the next three days he was careful not to let Duval see him. He could tell when Duval believed he had shaken off pursuit. Although he was slumping in the saddle from fatigue, Duval rode a little more confidently now, without looking back over his shoulder as often as before.

That third night, Duval, obviously totally worn out, made camp by the side of a small, fast-running stream. He turned in late, after midnight, probably figuring that even if anyone was following him, the night would mask where he had stopped. There was only a quarter moon, but that, and the stars, plus the power of Raider's field glasses, had kept Duval in sight all the time. Moving in close on foot, Raider watched the other man wolf down a cold meal. Duval might feel more secure tonight, but he still wasn't risking a fire.

But he'd risked something even greater—the fast little stream. It roared down over a rocky bed, its noise loud enough to drown out most other sounds. Raider watched Duval spread out his bedroll, climb into it, and go to sleep. He continued to watch for a couple of hours, to make certain Duval was deeply asleep, then he started in, on foot, moving quietly.

The noise of the stream made it easy. Nevertheless, Raider moved in slowly, carefully. Within an hour he was only ten yards away from his sleeping quarry. He waited there for another half hour, watching, listening. By now dawn was near; the eastern sky was beginning to lighten. Able to make out more detail now, Raider saw that Duval had left his rifle leaning against a tree about a yard from his head. And his pistol was outside the bedroll, still in its holster. True, it was only inches from Duval's right hand, but it should have been inside the bedroll with him, which is the way Raider would have played it.

Raider slowly and carefully moved the pistol and rifle out of reach. Duval's knife was nowhere in sight, but it usually wasn't anyhow. It was probably inside the bedroll. Fine.

Now that Duval's firearms were out of the way, Raider stood up straight and walked over to a rock about ten yards from Duval, where he sat down, facing the sleeping man. Duval, used to sleeping late, and exhausted to boot, was showing no signs of waking up, even though it was fully light now. The sun would be up in another fifteen minutes.

Raider began pitching small pebbles toward the quiet form. Duval grunted, and with his eyes still closed, swung his arms angrily, as if batting at flies. A pebble caught him on the cheek. His eyes opened halfway, wandered around the campsite . . . then flew wide open as he saw Raider.

"Mornin', Ernie," Raider said pleasantly. "My, you sure are one for sleepin'."

Duval's right hand groped for his pistol. Raider held up Duval's gunbelt. "Lookin' for something?" He tossed the gunbelt far into the brush. The rifle followed.

Duval started to sit up. Raider had his own pistol in his hand now. The hard snick of the hammer being cocked sounded clearly even above the noise of the stream. Duval froze. "About time we had us a little talk," Raider said, having to raise his voice a little so that it would carry above the sound of the water.

Duval remained still. He was obviously wondering why Raider hadn't already shot him, and more importantly, when he would. But if Raider wanted to put it off by talking, he'd be glad to let him talk.

"Surprised to see you doin' so poorly," Raider said. "I kinda figured that you had it all figured out that Van de Witt was going to make you a rich man."

"Van de Witt?" Duval replied. "Oh. You mean the boss."

"Yeah. The boss."

"That son of a bitch!" Duval said, venom in his voice. "He only give me a couple of thousand bucks. Then one night when I got drunk, him an' Jackson took off with all the rest of the loot."

"That's the last you saw of them?"

"Yeah. An' if I ever see 'em again, they're dead men."

Raider smiled. It was not a very nice smile. "But we know that's not gonna happen, don't we, Ernie. 'Cause you ain't gonna see them again. You ain't ever gonna see anybody again. 'Cause it's you that's the dead man."

Raider raised the pistol, pointed it at Duval, who flinched away. He was still in his bedroll, and his hands had dipped down inside it. Raider knew what he held there, and he knew that Duval would make his move soon, even if it was a doomed one. He had no choice.

But Duval's timetable was thrown off when Raider suddenly lowered the hammer of his .44 and laid it down behind the rock on which he was sitting. Duval was too surprised to move. Then Raider stood up. He reached toward the back of his belt and pulled out his big bowie. "Time to finish it, Ernie," he said quietly.

A look of joyful incredulity passed over Duval's face, and then he was out of the bedroll, springing to his feet, the wicked blade he always carried grasped in his right hand, as Raider had known it would be. "You stupid sucker," Duval snickered, bouncing on the balls of his feet. "You're the one that's a dead man!"

The two men faced one another. Raider planted himself solidly, the huge bowie held loosely out in front of him. Duval was more the panther, the stalker, circling around the bigger man and his bigger knife, fluid, deadly, threatening.

Duval lunged forward, his knife aimed at Raider's stomach. Raider moved to parry, but Duval's move had been a fake, and he leaped a little to one side, the tip of his knife flicking out quickly, drawing blood from Raider's left forearm. Duval could probably have pushed his advantage and hurt Raider worse, but he was enjoying himself too much to rush things. "So . . . you figured you had to play it fair," he snickered. "Had to do it the hero's way, give me an even chance. Well, you big stupid lump o' dog shit, it ain't even at all, 'cause I'm gonna cut you up into little strips an' give you to the nearest Injuns to be dried into jerky meat."

Raider said nothing. He remained standing solidly, a thin trickle of blood running down his left arm, his knife steady in front of his body. He let Duval prance around some more, then he suddenly moved forward, more quickly than such a big man should have been able to move. Duval was so busy talking that he was partially taken by surprise, and before he knew what was happening, Raider's heavier blade had beaten his lighter one aside and the broad tip of the bowie had sliced through his shirt, cutting a shallow groove across his chest.

"Son of a bitch!" Duval cursed, dodging away, his knife slashing the air close to Raider's eyes, forcing him to halt his advance.

The playing was over now, the fight was on in earnest, but neither man could quite seem to break through the other's guard. So Duval began to taunt his opponent, hoping to make him angry, to trick him into losing control. And he taunted him with the one thing that would hurt him most—with Sarah's death.

"Oh, she was one hell of a fighter," Duval said, an ugly little grin twisting his mouth. "Kept kickin' an' squirmin' even after it was in her. An' I ain't talking about my knife, though that was in her a little later, too. Damn. Never thought a woman could have so much blood in her."

Raider's face remained impassive, so Duval danced nearer, searching for more words, when Raider suddenly sprang again. Duval, too close, half staggered back, his left hand held out for balance. Raider's bowie swung in a short hard arc, cutting all four fingers from Duval's left hand, just behind the second knuckle. Duval staggered away, out of range, staring down at white bone, pink flesh. The razor-sharp bowie had left clean stumps. They were bleeding, the blood running down into Duval's palm, as he stared at what was left of his hand.

And now he was the one who lost control; he'd never before been cut badly in a knife fight. "You sack o' shit!" he screamed, lunging forward, slashing wildly. And now Raider began to whittle him down, slashing surgically, opening up deep long cuts on his arms, his thighs, across his forehead so that blood ran down into his eyes, half blinding him.

Knowing that he was in great danger, that loss of blood would soon weaken him so much that he wouldn't be able to defend himself, Duval put the last of his energy into one final attack, lunging forward, his blade drawing blood again, this time from Raider's knife arm, a shallow cut, and then he drove in deep, aiming the long slender tip of his blade upward, at a point just below Raider's sternum, thrusting hard.

Raider blocked the thrust with the bowie, and as Duval's knife arm was forced back, he seized it with his left hand. And now he was free to move inside, the bowie driving forward with great power, most of its fourteen inches sinking deep into Duval's belly. Duval shuddered from the shock of it, his eyes opening wide in amazement; he was horribly aware of all that steel inside his body. The two men stood toe to toe for a few seconds, Duval shuddering from head to foot, then Raider suddenly twisted the bowie and ripped it sideways, hard, opening a huge wound in Duval's abdomen. Duval did not cry out until the knife had left his body, and then he screamed, a high thin sound, and he slowly bent forward, trying to hold in his guts as they spilled from his body. He sank to his knees with his hands full of his own intestines, his face twisted with the horror of it. Raider stood back, watching his enemy as he knelt before him. "Doesn't feel too good when it's happening to you, does it, Ernie," he murmured.

Duval remained on his knees, seemingly afraid to move. Raider walked over, picked up his pistol, and put it back in its holster. One last look at Duval, then he walked away into the trees, toward his horse. He had only gone about halfway when he heard the first horrible, agonized screams coming from the campsite. Raider kept walking, reached his horse, swung up into the saddle. The screams were intensifying. He headed the horse toward the trail, the screams following.

Even after he had ridden about half a mile he could still hear the screams. He stopped his horse, sitting motionless in the saddle. The screams were sinking a little in volume now, the sound lower, more guttural. He suddenly pulled his horse around and went galloping back toward the clearing.

Ernie Duval was still on his knees when Raider reached him, but his hands were now down at his sides, his intestines trailing to the ground in front of him. He looked up dully as Raider rode closer. Hope kindled in his eyes as he saw Raider reach for his pistol. "Please . . ." he murmured, his voice almost unrecognizable. "Hurts . . . so much . . ."

Raider shot him between the eyes. The impact of the 250-grain bullet knocked Duval over onto his back, his legs still doubled beneath him. His body twitched several times, then lay still. Raider set the Remington on half-cock, opened the loading gate, and used the ejector rod to punch out the empty shell casing. One last look down at what was left of Ernie Duval as he pushed home a fresh round, then he holstered the pistol, spun his mount, and rode away. And as he rode he wondered why he didn't feel any better. Why what he had just done had not brought Sarah back to him.

# CHAPTER SEVENTEEN

The chase after Ernie Duval had taken Raider nearly to the Utah border. Salt Lake City was only another three days' ride, so he immediately headed south. The land was a little kinder here, softening slightly compared to the area where Duval lay dead, a meal for scavengers.

Once in Salt Lake, Raider telegraphed the Chicago office. He informed Pinkerton of Ernie Duval's demise and requested information about Breaker Jackson or John Van de Witt.

Pinkerton's reply arrived two days later. It seemed that Breaker Jackson had been up to his old tricks again, robbing banks, express offices, and any other places that might have a little money, this time down in West Texas.

Raider immediately went to a livery stable and sold the big bay for twenty dollars, which was as much as he was worth in his present condition. The trailsman in him wanted to buy another horse, and perhaps a pack animal, and head south immediately. There was some beautiful scenery down that way—the canyon country of southeast Utah, a wonderfully empty land of bizarrely sculpted sand-

stone and shale, and beyond that the Taos area of New
Mexico. Tempting. Ride and ride, and maybe try to forget
a little. But he couldn't do it, he had to hurry, there was no
time. Not if he was going to catch up to Breaker Jackson
and John Van de Witt and make them pay.

But why was it, then, that from time to time he could
swear he heard Sarah whispering into his ear, whispering
weakening words, urging him to forget this vendetta, to
forget her, to learn to live for himself again.

Raider was on the train that afternoon, traveling east,
heading once again for Cheyenne. Strange, how the pursuit
of Van de Witt and his gang kept taking him through
Cheyenne. Not that he had much choice. From where he
was, the rail line to Cheyenne was the quickest way around
the enormous obstacle of the Rocky Mountains.

From Cheyenne, he took the train to Denver. It was less
than a day's trip. Flat dry plains stretched away to the east,
mountains rose in the west, the Front Range, hanging over
Denver like an enormous jagged wall. Before changing
trains in Denver, Raider considered checking in with
McParland at the Denver office, but decided not to lose the
time. The telegram from Chicago had told him all he
wanted to know—that at least one of the remaining two
men he was after might possibly be found to the south, in
West Texas.

It was a beautiful time of the year to be in the mountains—late September. The aspens and cottonwoods in
their fall plumage made bright swatches of color against
the dark green of the conifers. Nice to stop and rest, lay up
for a while, but he had to press on. There was always the
chance that someone else would get to Jackson first.

After rising high into the Colorado mountains, the rail
dipped down through Raton Pass, which in Spanish mean
Mouse Pass, and then headed into New Mexico. The rail
didn't continue much farther; for the past several years the
Santa Fe Railroad had been fighting with the Denver and
Rio Grande Railroad over the right-of-way into New Mexico. Each company took turns hiring gunmen to harass the

other's work camps. Meanwhile, little roadbed was laid. The rails ended just short of Santa Fe.

From the railhead, Raider traveled by stage to Santa Fe. He liked this country—high, dry, clean plateau. The little pueblo had not changed much since the Spanish had founded it more than two hundred years before. Flat-roofed, whitewashed adobe buildings sat stolidly in the bright New Mexican sun, blending in with the dun-colored landscape. Aspens and cottonwoods grew wherever there was a little water. The air was clear and clean, the way Raider liked it.

The population was a mixture of Spanish and Pueblo Indian, with an overlay of Anglos. The atmosphere seemed peaceful. Not having rested for several days, Raider took a room in a small hotel. After eating a huge meal that seemed to be designed mostly around chile peppers, he repaired to his room late in the afternoon, belching fire. It had been a hot day, and the room was still very warm. He lay half asleep on the narrow cot that was the room's main item of furniture, looking up at the dark old beams that stretched across the whitewashed ceiling. He was vaguely aware of a guitar strumming softly somewhere else in the building, of the soft sound of Spanish outside the window, of the sense of agelessness around him. Once again, the thought of stopping, of going no further, seemed tempting, but only for a moment. He promised himself, just before drifting off to sleep, that he would not listen, that he would continue on, that he would avenge Sarah.

He had purchased a fine big black stallion the day before for fifty dollars. He was at the livery stable, saddling up, an hour before dawn. He rode out of town just as the first promise of light began to show in the eastern sky. The light grew quickly, as it does in high dry places, coloring the sky a marvelous light mauve color that faded to white minutes before the sun, blazing with amazing purity, moved above the distant, sharply etched horizon.

His route lay southeast, with the morning sun positioned ahead of his left shoulder. The trail soon led downwards out of the high country. Within a day and a half he was in hot, barren land, the sere brushy New Mexico desert. He had been warned before leaving Santa Fe to watch out for Apaches. Nahche, old Cochise's son, along with a young buck named Geronimo, were out raiding, the worst outbreak of Indian trouble in the territory since Cochise himself had been planted.

Raider saw no living Apaches. However, late one afternoon, noticing a smudge of smoke on the horizon, he rode in that direction to investigate. Half an hour later his field glasses showed the smoking wreckage of a cabin, about half a mile away. He scouted the cabin slowly, riding toward it in an oblique circle. Satisfied that there were no signs of life, he finally rode in.

All that was left of the cabin were the stumps of its adobe walls. The bodies of a white man and woman and a little girl were grouped together behind a low rock wall. Riding closer, Raider saw many brass cartridge cases lying on the ground around the bodies. There were no signs of torture, so he figured that the man, probably with ammo running low, must have shot his wife and daughter, then turned the gun on himself. Understandable, considering what they would have faced if Apaches had captured them alive—particularly the females. There was little doubt that it had been Apaches. All three bodies had been scalped.

Raider found a shovel in a little shed behind the house. The shed had been looted, of course, the shovel was one of the few items remaining. It had a broken handle, but it was enough of a shovel for Raider to dig two shallow graves. He'd been digging a lot of graves lately.

He placed the man in one grave, the woman and the little girl in the other. He had just started to fill in the graves when he heard animals snarling back in the brush. Investigating, he found the body of an Apache lying about forty yards from the ruined cabin. Apparently the dead settler had managed to hit at least one of his attackers.

Four coyotes were fighting over the body. Raider hesitated, leaning on the shovel, thinking about digging another hole. Then he shrugged and headed back toward the graves, leaving the dead man to the coyotes. He didn't like Apaches; he had seen too much of their work.

Raider's destination was a sparsely populated and utterly barren section of West Texas, a day's ride or so west of Pecos. By the time he reached it he felt as if he'd been riding over flat, dull brushlands for a hundred years. Every which way he looked the land was exactly the same—featureless.

Finally, in a barren little town out on the edge of nowhere, he found what he was looking for—the posse hunting Breaker Jackson. It was led by one of the hardest-looking sheriffs Raider had ever met, one Jeremiah Hodges. Hodges was not terribly happy to see a Pinkerton operative, maybe competition for the reward money. Raider came right out with it, because he knew there would be absolutely no chance of pulling off the same kind of trick he'd pulled off with that sheriff in Kansas, over the Simes brothers' reward. You didn't even *try* that kind of thing with a man like Sheriff Jeremiah Hodges.

Hodges described Breaker Jackson's latest foray. "Him an' his bunch robbed a bank over Odessa way. A real shoot-em'-up kinda job. Lead flyin' everywhere, people runnin' for cover, lots of hollerin' an' people pissin' in their pants, an' the damned fools on'y got away with maybe five hundred dollars at the most. Don't bother me none, though, that it was only five hundred dollars. We'll hang 'em just as high as if it'd been five thousand."

"You sure it was Jackson?" Raider asked.

"Yep. We caught one of·'em. He told us Breaker Jackson was leadin' the bunch. That waddie told us a lot o' things 'fore he had his accident."

"Accident?"

The sheriff's mouth twitched, the closest thing to a grin Raider would see on his face for the several days he knew him. "Yep. Accident. Fell off a box he was standin' on, an' the rope around his neck kinda did him in. Real clumsy man. Any man who robs banks around my bailiwick has gotta be clumsy."

"You sure that Jackson wasn't just along for the ride?

That maybe another man might have been leadin' the gang. A tall, well-dressed dude, wearin' a mask?"

"Nope. Just Jackson an' those yahoos with him. A real passel o' losers, more likely to shoot off their own toes than to pull a nice clean bank robbery."

Which Raider had already pretty much figured. If the raid had been led by Van de Witt, it would have gone off a lot more smoothly than it obviously had. He'd only asked out of a lingering hope that it might all end here, right now.

Jackson's gang had left a wide trail. The sheriff, leading a posse of a dozen men, was about to set out after them. He made no objection when Raider asked to come along. "Why not?" Hodges replied, shrugging. "You Pinks can get a good look at how we Texans take care of bad apples."

They rode out immediately. Raider doubted he had ever ridden with a harder-looking bunch, harder even than the boss's gang. They *rode* hard, too. Within a day and a half they had considerably cut down the distance between themselves and the gang. The bandits' trail led toward the west.

"Probably tryin' to make it to El Paso, then down into Mexico and the easy life," Hodges said laconically. "I wired ahead. They won't be able to get through that way."

The next day the posse reached the tiny settlement of Van Horn. The landscape had turned into low, barren hills, but the hills had a certain charm about them, particularly after the boredom of that endless barren plain. Van Horn itself was mostly a collection of adobes, with a couple of frame structures built by well-off Anglos. It was there that a posse riding east had clashed with Jackson's gang. Four of the bandits had been killed, cutting their numbers down to six or seven. The survivors had ridden off due south, toward the border, which was only twenty or thirty miles away.

"Okay, boys, lets push it hard," Hodges curtly told his men.

The bandits' trail now led south through the Van Horn Mountains. It was much more difficult land, a rough trail to ride. There was very little water, so each man had to make his water last. And it was hot, the eternal heat of southern Texas. The ground being so broken, tracking the fleeing bandits became a problem, and here Raider earned the approbation of Sheriff Hodges by picking up traces of the bandits' trail when no one else could. Hodges never said anything openly, but Raider was aware of his approval.

They spotted the bandits just before dark, seven of them, riding weary horses about a mile ahead. The chase was on, the possemen spurring their only slightly less weary mounts into greater speed. The bandits had spotted their pursuers by now, and were doing their best to get away, but the distance between the two groups slowly lessened, narrowing to gunshot range just as the light began to go.

The bandits tried to put up a fight; they knew they were as good as dead if captured. And soon most of them were. One after the other, they were shot out of their saddles, until it became too dark to aim. By then, only two of the bandits were left, obviously the two with the best horses. They rode off into the darkness. Raider was sure Jackson was one of them.

"Let's hold up here, boys," Sheriff Hodges sang out.

"What the hell for?" Raider demanded. The fleeing men were only a few hundred yards away. Even in the dark the possemen could fan out, box them in. Raider was anxious to get moving. He was sure one of the fleeing men was Breaker Jackson.

"I kinda figure that Mexico lies just a little bit ahead," Hodges said. "Here's where I gotta stop."

Seeing the disbelieving look on Raider's face, Hodges chose to add, "Got myself into a passel o' trouble last year, chasin' some hardcases over the border. The Mex's have got 'em a real touchy governor down in that part of Chihuahua. He'd be on the telegraph to Washington in a flash if he caught me at it again."

"So you can't go in?" Raider asked.

"Nope."

"Well, I sure as hell can."

"Yep. Reckon you can, all right. You're more or less a private citizen."

Raider immediately wheeled his horse and began to ride on south after Jackson and the other man—alone. He heard Hodges call out after him, "I'd watch yourself down there if I was you. They don't take too kindly to gringos."

Raider never turned, just kept riding straight south, toward Mexico.

# CHAPTER EIGHTEEN

Fifteen minutes later Raider reached the Rio Grande. The river was quite shallow here, although rather broad. He crossed it without difficulty. He was now in Mexico.

It had grown very dark. There was no sign of the men he was chasing, nor, in the darkness, could he make out their tracks. The moon had not yet risen, and since the sky was overcast, there was no starshine. He considered dismounting and striking matches in an attempt to locate the fugitives' tracks, but realized that doing so would only pinpoint his own position if the men he was following were out there somewhere in the darkness, waiting to see if the posse was still on their trail.

Raider decided to strike out in the direction in which it was most logical the fugitives had gone—deeper into Mexico. Traveling slowly, always alert for sign, or for any sound that might alert him to an ambush, he headed a little west of south.

The moon didn't rise until sometime after midnight. The cloud cover had thinned considerably, and the moon, although only half full, gave enough light for Raider to begin making out details of the surrounding countryside. For the most part the land was quite barren, sandy and brushy, the ground soft enough to give indications if anyone had recently passed this way, but he saw nothing, no sign at all of tracks. For all he knew he was riding straight away from the men he was after. Finally, he decided that the most intelligent course would be to get some rest, then begin the hunt in earnest the next morning.

He made a cold camp, lying down fully clothed on the soft sandy soil, his horse's reins looped around his wrist, his rifle lying across his body, his right hand near the butt of his pistol. When he awoke, it was beginning to grow light. He stood up, slightly stiff, pulled some dried meat from his saddlebags, and mounted, slowly chewing the hard, tasteless, but nourishing food as he rode.

He headed back the way he had come, toward the point where he had lost Jackson and the other man in the dark. He finally cut across their trail about half a mile from the Rio Grande. They were heading southeast! If he had continued riding in the direction he'd earlier taken, he would only have been putting more distance between himself and Jackson.

The tracks led straight on. The amount of sand the steady wind had blown into the hoofprints indicated that the riders must have passed this way several hours before. Raider pushed on, and by the middle of the afternoon he saw a small pueblo in the distance, a collection of adobe shacks and sagging corrals. The tracks led straight into the town.

Raider, keeping out of sight by riding through little arroyos that had been made by flash floods, circled partway around the town. He saw tracks leading out the other side. Apparently Jackson and his companion had ridden straight on through.

Raider decided to enter the town. He had eaten the last of his jerky; perhaps he could buy some supplies, and maybe replenish his water. That is, if the town had anything at all to offer. It was a miserable little place, obviously dirt poor. People seemed in short supply. A couple of men were taking their afternoon siestas, propped up against adobe walls, with their big sombreros tipped down over their faces. Raider spotted a cantina halfway down the single dusty track that was the town's main street. He hitched his horse outside, then headed toward the door, which was really not a door but just a piece of ragged cloth drawn over an irregular rectangular opening in the building's thick adobe wall.

As usual, when Raider entered an unknown room, he quickly slipped to the side, out of the light, the moment he was through the door. Besides the bartender, there was only one man inside, an old fellow in ragged clothes, half lying on the bar, a glass of mescal tipped over next to his right hand.

The bartender, a thin, dried-up little man, looked disinterestedly in Raider's direction. "You got any beer? *Cerveza?* Raider asked.

The bartender nodded, then produced a dusty bottle of beer. Raider pulled out a handful of silver. The bartender took fifteen cents. The price seemed a little steep to Raider, but he wanted the beer.

It tasted a great deal better than the dusty, chipped condition of the bottle's exterior had promised. Raider remembered that the Mexicans usually made damned good beer. Standing at the bar, he drank down the first bottle in two long pulls, then bought another, which he took to a small table near the back of the room. He picked that particular table because there was a big sideboard and a jumble of heavy wooden furniture nearby, and a door not far beyond. Cover. Just in case.

He asked the bartender if there was anything to eat. The bartender nodded, then called out toward a doorway behind the bar. A woman appeared, as fat as the bartender was thin. The tone of their conversation suggested to Raider that the two were married. The bartender said something to her about food, and fifteen minutes later the woman reappeared with a plate of tamales, fried beans, and tortillas, which she placed in front of Raider.

As she turned away, heading back in the direction from

which she had come, the bartender brushed past her. *"Treinta centavos,"* he told Raider.

Raider paid him the thirty cents, then waded into the food. It was damned good. The tamales were full of meat; the cornmeal was cooked just right, not too dry, not too wet. The food was fiery hot, but Raider, having spent most of his life in the West, liked it that way. The second bottle of beer helped quench some of the flames. He was beginning to like this place. It was a little short on meaningful conversation, but a man could get plenty to eat and drink.

Once he had finished eating, he would, of course, ask the bartender about two other gringos who had passed through town a little earlier. He was mopping up the last of the beans with a piece of tortilla, trying to phrase his rusty Spanish in his mind, when the curtain covering the doorway was pushed aside, and three men came inside. For a moment the daylight behind them blinded Raider, but as they came further into the room, he saw that all three were Mexicans.

Gunmen, all of them. These were no vaqueros, no cowpunchers. They were dressed in rather ragged but show-off clothing—fancy embroidered vests, tight *charro* pants, huge broad-brimmed sombreros. Their boots jingled with big spurs, the rowels so large that they dragged on the floor. And the newcomers were armed to the teeth, each man carrying two pistols and at least one knife. Banditos, sure enough.

They swaggered into the bar as if they owned it, which, in a way, they did. In such an isolated area, their heavy armament would be enough to get them anything they wanted—until someone harder and meaner came along.

Of course they noticed Raider, but after one contemptuous glance, chose to ignore him. They turned toward the bar, and, to a man, ordered tequila, a rich man's drink in a town as poor as this. They were talking loudly together, and to the bartender, and Raider was aware that the word "gringo" was very prominent in their conversation. Raider noticed that the old drunk slumped over the bar had wakened. After a good look at his new drinking companions, he prudently got up and staggered out the door. The bartender, too, tended to shrink back toward the doorway leading to the cantina's back rooms.

Raider finished the last of his beans. He was just pushing the plate away when one of the Mexicans turned around to face him. He was the biggest of the three, a rather handsome man, with thick black hair and a large drooping mustache. He pushed his sombrero back a little on his head and smiled in Raider's direction. It was actually more of a sneer than a smile. He said something in Spanish that Raider chose to ignore. So he switched to English. "'Ey, gringo. "I ast you what you are doing down here, in our country. You lost?"

Raider remained seated, looking up at the man but saying nothing. This hombre was undoubtedly the leader of this little group, or at least considered himself so. His clothing and gear were the most fancy. His vest would have been quite elegant if not for the food stains on the front. He carried twin pearl-handled Colt forty-fives in a double belt rig that crisscrossed his body just below the waist. Raider reflected that the weight of all the ammo stuffed into the bullet loops on those gunbelts must really weigh the man down.

The man took a few steps toward Raider, still grinning. Raider continued to sit, although he hitched his right leg a little to the side, so that he would be able to reach his .44 more quickly, if it came to that. The Mexican saw the movement, and his mocking smile faded a little. It faded a great deal more when he looked into Raider's eyes and saw no sign of fear there at all, only a calm, deadly concentration.

Raider was not particularly worried about the big Mexican or his companions. To men like them, opportunistic bandits who spent most of their time squeezing small men like the bartender, three against one would probably not seem desirable odds. Already, the look on the big man's face indicated that he would like to find some graceful way out of the situation into which his braggadocio had landed him.

He might have found it if the door curtains hadn't opened again, admitting two more men. After another moment of light-blindness, Raider saw who they were. Breaker Jackson and another gringo.

Careful not to move too quickly, Raider sat up straighter in his chair. He was now faced with a threat of a considerably higher caliber. He wondered what Jackson was doing here; he supposedly had ridden right on out the other side of town. Raider cursed himself for not having checked their tracks, for having been too eager for beer and food to take the time to make certain that the hoofprints going out of town matched the ones coming in. It could have been anybody riding out the far side.

"Well, well, well," Jackson said, smiling at Raider. "Speak of the devil, an' damn if he don't show up."

That was the second insincere smile Raider had received in the last five minutes. He did not smile back. "Afternoon, Jackson," he said coolly.

"Yeah. Your last." It was said with no apparent rancor, almost cheerfully.

"That's what Ernie Duval tried to tell me too," Raider replied. "Only it didn't quite turn out the way he'd planned it."

Jackson's eyebrows raised. "You did for Ernie? Well, he always was more bark than bite."

"Van de Witt," Raider asked. "Is he with you?"

Jackson shook his head. "Uh-uh. A big man like him, used to all that good livin', don't take too kindly to ridin' the outlaw trail when he can't just mosey on home to his little wifey an' sweet kiddies at the end of a hard day's work robbin' banks."

"Where'd he head?"

Jackson shrugged. "San Francisco, I think. If he had any brains, he'd leave the fuckin' country, like I just did. Only I kinda think he hates makin' it permanent, leavin' his wife and sweet kiddies for good and ever. Why you askin? You figure you'll live long enough to ride on after him?"

"All in good time, Jackson. You're next on my list . . .

before Van de Witt, after Ernie. I owe you one. More than one . . . for what you did., You and Duval and Van de Witt."

Jackson laughed. "To the girl? Yeah, I guess you'd feel that way. The boss figured doin' something like that would kinda get under your skin. He's a real thinker. Well, it turned out to be a lot of fun, all right. But . . . speaking o' owing people, I figure I owe you one too."

And now Breaker Jackson's voice lowered into a deadly snarl. "You lyin' sack o' shit. Playin' your Pinkerton tricks on me. I'm gonna take you apart real slow. Maybe a bullet through the knee, an' then finish you off with my hands."

There was a fair probability of him doing just that. His companion, a man Raider had never seen before, but one hell of a mean-looking son of a bitch, was posted over by the door. If he and Jackson both threw down on Raider at the same time, they'd have him in a cross fire. And then there were the Mexicans. The odds were now more to their liking—five against one. They apparently knew Jackson, and if so, they would know the quality of the help backing them up.

Which is probably what prompted the big one with the pearl-handled Colts to make his move. That, and the huge burden of machismo he carried around with him, a load that would force him to prove his manhood again and again until the day he died.

Which came much sooner than he had expected. He stepped forward, grinning again. "Now, gringo pig, maybe you gonna talk to me, no?"

"Nope," Raider replied, grinning back. The Mexican had stepped right in front of him, blocking Raider off from both Breaker Jackson and his man by the door.

"Get the hell outta the way, Juan!" Jackson shouted, but by then it was too late. Juan already had his hand on his gun butt, but his mouth fell open in surprise when he realized that somehow Raider's .44 was already in his hand. His mouth fell open even further when the .44 bellowed and a heavy slug took him low in the chest, throwing him back toward Jackson, further spoiling Jackson's view of Raider.

Raider was already out of his chair, rolling to the side. He was not in position to fire at Jackson, and Jackson was in no position to fire at him, so Raider opened up on the banditos by the bar, killing both of them with three bullets. They went down, screaming, even as Juan continued to topple, clawing at Jackson as he fell, further tying him up.

Raider rolled behind the héavy furniture near his table. A bullet chipped wood inches from his head as Jackson's man took a shot at him. Raider fired back, his bullet raking the man's shoulder, causing him to duck for cover. A moment later Raider had reached the rear door he had so thoughtfully positioned himself close to. Then he was outside, with Breaker Jackson's bullets gouging wood splinters from the door frame behind him.

"Get the hell after him!" Jackson screamed at his companion. "I'll go around the other way."

"Uh-uh. Not through that door. I don't wanna get my ass shot off."

"You gutless bastard! He's outta ammo!"

Which was the truth. Like almost everyone who didn't fancy shooting his leg off, Raider carried only five rounds in his Remington, with an empty space under the hammer. He'd used up every damned one of those five rounds in the bar, and he was fumbling to reload now, as he ran toward the cover of an adobe building twenty yards away. He didn't waste time reloading every chamber; he punched out one empty, shoved in a live round, then spun the cylinder five clicks to the left, positioning that one loaded cylinder into firing position.

Jackson's man had come running out through the door after Raider, gratified that no lead had as yet come his way. As Raider had been, he was blinded by the bright outdoor light, but he recovered quickly enough to see Raider ducking around the side of the adobe. He ran forward, firing rapidly, his bullets gouging out chunks of adobe. He was trying to make it around the corner of the building before Raider reached better cover.

And he ran right into Raider, who had stopped, turned, cocked his piece, waited, and then put a bullet into the gunman's throat from only three feet away.

Leaving the man gurgling out the last of his life on the ground, Raider moved around to the back of the building, furiously shucking empties from his pistol and shoving in new rounds. He'd heard Jackson say he was heading around to the other side, and sure enough, here he came, pistol in hand, running fast, bent low to the ground.

He was a lot smarter than his late companion, and spotted Raider just as Raider spotted him. Jackson dived forward behind the cover of a horse watering trough half a second before Raider opened fire, his own pistol sending lead in Raider's direction. That man can shoot, Raider thought grimly, as Jackson's bullets drove him back behind the adobe.

It became a game of cat and mouse for a while, as each man stalked the other, knowing that showing too much of himself would probably get a hole blown in him. They dodged through the town, sniping at one another, each man attempting to set up an ambush that would surprise the other. No one interrupted them. Perhaps this godforsaken little *pueblito* was used to wild gunfights.

It couldn't go on forever, and it didn't. Raider and Jackson finally bushwhacked one another at just the same moment, each startling the other so thoroughly that they both foolishly wasted ammunition. It happened just outside a small *tienda* that stocked farm and ranch implements. Their ammunition spent, each man heard the hammer of his pistol click down onto a spent primer. Raider recovered first, and sprinted across the twenty or so yards separating him from Jackson, reaching for the big bowie he always carried toward the rear of his belt, only to discover that it was no longer there; somehow it had been lost during the fight.

But he couldn't stop now, he was so close, and to turn and head in another direction would give Jackson, who was desperately trying to reload, a chance to shoot him in the back. So Raider continued his forward rush, crashing into Jackson so hard that the other man dropped his pistol.

They grappled hand to hand, and now Raider remembered how Jackson had gotten his nickname, Breaker; he liked to beat men to death with his bare hands. Which he was trying to do now, attempting to slam a fist into Raider's throat, trying to get his knee up into his groin. He was very strong; Raider realized he had to keep him tied up, occupied. He drove his head into Jackson's chest, slamming him backwards against the door of the little *tienda*. The door, flimsy from decades of dry rot, fell off its leather hinges, and both men stumbled into the interior of the shop.

Jackson broke away first, his right hand thrusting into a pile of pick handles, scattering them everywhere as his fingers closed around one of the hard wooden shafts.

He started toward Raider, the pick handle raised above his head, a look of murderous triumph lighting up his eyes. But Raider slipped under the blow that Jackson was aiming at his head, a blow that would have split his skull if it had connected.

Fortunately, in his haste to secure one of the pick handles for himself, Jackson had scattered the rest all over the room. Raider, stumbling away from Jackson and heading toward the door, scooped one up, grateful for the smooth cool feel of the hickory against his palm.

Raider stumbled out into the street, caught his balance, then turned to face the *tienda* just as Jackson crashed through the remains of the door, pick handle held over his head, ready to kill.

He stopped when he saw Raider waiting for him with another pick handle raised high. A prudent man didn't rush in on a pick handle held in the hands of a strong man, not without giving it a hell of a lot of thought. Raider had the same reaction. The two men began to circle one another cautiously, the pick handles held out in front of them as each looked for an opening.

They suddenly seemed to come together, almost as if by prearrangement, pick handles swinging hard, each man intent on ending it now. The pick handles glinted in the sun as they were swung repeatedly. Each man managed to parry most of the blows, or the fight would have been over much sooner, but each man also scored hits. Panting, bloodied, hurting, they continued to go after one another, evenly matched, until Raider remembered what Jackson had said in the cantina, his comments about what he and the others had done to Sarah, how much he had enjoyed it, and now a mad killing rage swept over Raider, a red mist of fury, and he charged in, oblivious to pain, to danger, wanting only to kill.

First he broke Jackson's left arm. As Jackson staggered back, gasping in agony, Raider continued forward. His pick handle smashed the fingers of Jackson's right hand, causing him to nearly drop his pick handle, and while he grimaced in pain, Raider broke several of the ribs on his left side.

After that, it was an execution, Raider's pick handle swinging in wide arcs, smashing the life out of Breaker Jackson. It was only toward the end that the red mist half obscuring Raider's vision began to clear and he was fully able to see what he had already done to the other man.

Jackson was shambling from side to side, weaponless now, his face battered almost beyond recognition, both arms broken, his kidneys pulped, one knee smashed, but somehow he remained on his feet. It was this, most of all, maybe courage, maybe only reflex blood-lust on Jackson's part, that cleared the rage from Raider's mind, and now he only wanted to end it. He raised his pick handle high, aiming at Jackson's head. Jackson didn't have the strength either to duck or to bring up his shattered arms. The broad, hard tip of the pick handle cracked against his forehead with the sound of a melon dropped on concrete, and now Jackson finally fell, his forehead split down the center, his eyes unfocused, staring off in different directions. He fell heavily. His arms and legs quivered for another few seconds, and then he lay still.

Raider shoved the bloody tip of the pick handle against the ground, leaning on it as he fought to regain his breath.

He prodded Breaker Jackson once with his toe. There was no movement. The man was dead. Another one for Sarah. More vengeance. An ugly vengeance. Raider wondered, as he wearily turned and headed for his horse, what Sarah would have thought, what she would have said, if *she* had been looking down at what was left of Breaker Jackson. He'd never know. There was no way he could ask her.

# CHAPTER NINETEEN

After southwest Texas and northern Chihuahua, San Francisco was another world—cool, lively, sophisticated. As he walked its crowded streets, Raider reflected that it had been his former partner, Doc's, favorite American city. And, of course, this is where he had planned to bring Sarah, if they had not . . .

After the fight with Breaker Jackson, Raider had headed straight for San Francisco. It was amazing how little time it had taken. The most difficult part of the trip had been the long ride back up into southern Texas, where he'd finally found rails. He had then taken the train north, back through Denver and Cheyenne, and then straight west, to California. The transcontinental railroad had been completed for more than ten years, but Raider still had difficulty getting used to how much it had changed travel in the West. Formerly, crossing the incredible barrier of the Sierras into California had been at the risk of one's life. Now, three or four days on a train, and then, California. Incredibly easy. But of course such ease of travel had its negative side. Now, every eastern tenderfoot would be able to make it out west without hardly trying. The land was going to fill up. The open spaces Raider loved would cease to exist.

At first Raider had hesitated about coming all the way out to San Francisco. There'd been only Breaker Jackson's casual mention that John Van de Witt *might* be in San Francisco, but the probability had turned into a near certainty, when, after telegraphing ahead to the Chicago office, Raider had learned that a man fitting Van de Witt's description had been seen in San Francisco. It had taken most of Raider's persuasive powers to convince his employers not to move in on the man, to wait until he had a chance to reach San Francisco and see for himself.

Raider still hurt from his fight with Breaker Jackson. Large purple bruises marked his arms, legs, and ribs. But he was alive, and Jackson wasn't. And now it would be Van de Witt's turn. The boss.

Raider was on the way to meet with the Pinkerton operative stationed in San Francisco who had first spotted Van de Witt. He was supposed to meet him way up on top of one of those damned hills. Damned if he'd walk. He heard the loud clanging of a bell. He turned and saw another wonder of the age just beginning to move up the hill. Breaking into a run, Raider leaped up onto the side platform of the cable car, then sat down, letting it climb the hill for him.

The last time he'd been here, Doc had to beg him to take the cable car; Raider hadn't wanted to pay the quarter fare. And as before, Raider was glad he had, not only because of the steepness of the grade, but also because of the magnificence of the view as the car neared the top of the hill. The immense blue expanse of the bay was spread out below him, farther than he could see. The docks, closer in, were thickly forested with the masts and funnels of numerous ships. In the distance, across the bay, the hills showed their usual dun autumn color. And all around him the city buzzed. It was a real city, not the usual jerry-built western-style collection of false-front buildings and seedy saloons. It was the only city Raider had ever seen that he liked.

After he got down from the cable car at the top of the hill, it was only a short walk to the small restaurant where he was to meet the Pinkerton operative. As Raider walked in the door, he spotted him seated at a rear table, a small nondescript man hunched over a schooner of beer. Raider sat down across from him. "Howdy, Charlie," he said, nodding.

Charlie grinned back at him, wiping beer froth from his mouth. "Howdy yourself. Glad to see you're still alive an' kickin', after runnin' around out in that fuckin' wilderness."

Raider smiled back. Charlie was a town operative; he had little use for the rigors of life on the trail, although more than once he'd gone after wanted men, chasing them through territory rougher than an old whore's tongue, cursing the hardships all the way, but doing it. "You hungry?" Charlie asked. When Raider nodded, he suggested the steaks. "They're good here, an' a steak is somethin' a man like you can understand."

Raider let the jibe pass. Doc used to poke at him the same way. He kind of missed it. He held his peace while the steaks were being prepared, but when Charlie continued to patter on about how good the food was in San Francisco, and how much he liked being here, Raider finally cut in. "Where can I find my man?"

A rather pained look passed over Charlie's normally good-natured face. "Well now, that might not be so easy."

"What the hell . . ." Raider growled, getting half out of his chair. "You haven't let him . . ."

"Now take it easy, Raider," Charlie said placatingly, and Raider finally realized why he had been so anxious to talk about other things. He was about to hear some bad news concerning Van de Witt.

"Come on, spit it out," he snarled.

"Well now, we think we know where he is," Charlie said hastily. "Well, we might know pretty close, anyhow."

"How close?"

"He may be up the coast a ways."

"How much of a ways?"

"About three hundred miles."

"Oh, fine."

Once he saw that Raider was not about to murder him, Charlie loosened up enough to tell the rest of the story. He had first got onto Van de Witt about a month before, when his attention had been drawn to a man whose face rang a bell in his head, even though he hadn't been able to say just why. "He sure didn't look like any bandit," Charlie said. "Hell, he was living at the Palace Hotel, which don't exactly cater to the bank robber type."

Raider nodded. The Palace was one of the newest and probably the most expensive hotel in the city. And big, with more than eight hundred rooms, and an enormous courtyard and a huge arched entranceway that wouldn't have looked out of place in a European palace. Yes, he could see a man like Van de Witt staying at the Palace.

"See, he'd grown a beard," Charlie continued. "It took me maybe three weeks to remember where I might've seen him—that wanted poster the agency put out. Anyhow, I'd been kind of keeping an eye on him, so I got to know a little about him, and it wasn't too pretty."

"How do you mean?"

"Well, you ever seen a man who was really trying to drink himself to death?"

Of course Raider had. But Van de Witt? The boss? The man of iron control who had run his gang like a Prussian general?

"No, no, it's true!" Charlie insisted. "He was juicin' it up bad, like there was somethin' really botherin' him, eatin' his guts out. An he was a mean drunk. They finally tossed him outta the Palace after he tried to do some pretty rough things to a chambermaid, then beat the shit outta the help when they got in the way. It was downhill fast after that. I mean, literally downhill. He

checked into a fleabag at the bottom of the hill, drinkin'
harder than ever."

"So why ain't he there now?"

Charlie looked uncomfortable. "It was my fault. Like
I said, I wasn't quite sure who he was. I had the wanted
poster by then, but with the beard . . . well . . . I wanted to
get good and close to make sure, I wanted to look right
past that beard. I thought I was being pretty careful
about it, but maybe he was sober that morning, an' spotted me. That's what I figure it had to be. I remember
him taking a good look at me, and then a couple of
hours later, when I came by with some help to take him
in—I was sure by then that it was Van de Witt—he was
gone. Lit right out."

Raider nodded. He was disappointed, but things like
this happened. "So?" he prompted.

"A gent who fits his description was seen gettin' on the
boat that goes up the coast to Eureka."

"You sure?"

"Well . . . sure enough."

Raider was happy to hear that the boat had already returned from its trip up north and was due to leave again
that afternoon. The boat was a little steam packet called the
*Coquille*. Raider was at the dock half an hour before sail-
ing time. Charlie, anxious to make up for losing Van de
Witt, had provided him with a five-dollar first-class ticket,
so Raider was comfortably ensconced in a deck chair when
the *Coquille* weighed anchor and started its long trip up the
coast.

The good news about Van de Witt's flight to the north
was that he had run to an area that was more or less a
one-way trap. Eureka was just about as isolated a place
as a man could find. The only really practical way to get
there was the way Raider was doing it. By boat. Inland,
and toward both the north and south, the land was an
inhospitable wilderness of mountain and forest. Some of
the roughest country in the West.

Raider sat on deck until it got dark. Mile after mile of
dark forest slid by, backed by steep mountains. And the

farther north they went, the darker the forest became, the rougher-looking the mountains. And the steeper the seas. This was not a soft land.

Late in the afternoon of the second day, they came in sight of Humboldt Bay. Eureka, journey's end, was located inside the bay, near the vast redwood forests that gave the little town its reason for existence. Over the past couple of hours Raider had begun to notice huge bald patches in the normally solid green of the forests. Lumbering. A thick cloud of smoke, dust, and debris hung over the huge bay, the foul breath of the lumber and pulp mills.

It was a pretty bay, and quite large, but badly silted up. A fellow passenger told Raider that the lumber interests had diverted the local rivers so that they could more easily float logs down into the bay, and that's what had silted it up. Progress.

Eureka was not a prepossessing town. It was a logger's town, made up mostly of featureless wooden buildings, with an occasional enormous gingerbread mansion for the logging aristocracy. The air was so thick it was difficult to breathe.

After disembarking, Raider checked into a small hotel, and then went out looking for Van de Witt. If Charlie was right, and Van de Witt was really trying to lose himself by crawling inside a bottle, the best place to look would be where there were lots of bottles.

Raider spent half the night wandering around the wetter parts of town, particularly the lower end of Two Street, which was what the locals called Second Street. Moving from saloon to saloon, Raider eventually found a few people who remembered Van de Witt.

"That son of a bitch drinks like a fish, an' he's mean as a snake when he gets drunk enough," one old rummy told Raider, grateful for the drink the Pinkerton bought him. "Kinda used up his welcome around here. Lit out up to the other side o' the bay."

It was too late by then to get a horse, so Raider went back to his room to get some sleep. He was up at dawn, knocking on the doors of the nearest livery stable. He bought a pretty good-looking animal with the understanding that the owner would buy it back at a profit when Raider was ready to leave. With his gear on the horse, including his Centennial, Raider rode out a little after sunup. If there was indeed a sun. The cloud of pollution from the mills made it difficult to tell.

As he rode farther north, the air cleared a little. The road curved around the east side of the bay. It was pretty land, or would have been pretty if it hadn't been for the devastation wreaked on it by the loggers. Whole mountainsides had been stripped of their trees. Usually, any debris remaining was burned, leaving little or no ground cover. Last year's rains had brought down mountains of mud, clogging streams, destroying the original land contours. Raider got the impression that the locals would be quite happy to destroy every living thing within sight, they'd willingly turn the entire area into a desert, if they could make plenty of money doing it.

It was only a six-or seven-mile ride around the bay to Arcata, the little town where Van de Witt was supposed to be staying. The devastation of the land began to put Raider into a despondent mood. This was probably going to be another day of killing. He was getting tired of killing. He knew he had been a little crazy when he'd killed Ernie Duval. It hadn't been quite so bad with Breaker Jackson. By then, the intensity of his grief over Sarah had begun to fade a little. The hatred had still been there, though, the desire for vengeance. But what about now? He felt played out. Not that he had any real regrets about the deaths of Duval and Jackson. He had decided when he first met them that they were men who needed killing. Time had not changed his opinion.

And what about Van de Witt? Strange, that a man like him could slide downhill so fast. But then, Raider had always sensed an air of madness about Van de Witt. He'd been playing a might strange game, living a double life: respected banker and loving father on the one hand, ruthless badlands bandit on the other. Maybe he'd finally split right down the middle when he could no longer play both roles.

Arcata was a much prettier town than Eureka. The center contained a neat little town square, complete with grass and flowers. Wetlands stretched away toward the west, in the direction of the sea. Steep mountains grew up out of the eastern edge of the town. It looked peaceful.

In such a small place, it took Raider only half an hour to find Van de Witt. The lobby of the little hotel where the fugitive was staying was so small as to be almost nonexistent. Raider was walking toward the door of Van de Witt's room when it opened and Van de Witt himself started to walk out through it. Raider's .44 was in the banker's gut, prodding him back inside the room, before he was fully aware of what was happening. Van de Witt staggered backward. The edge of the bed caught him behind the knees and he sat down heavily. "You!" he muttered, his voice hoarse.

"Yeah. Me."

Raider stood by the door, his .44 pointed at Van de Witt's chest. Van de Witt remained seated on the bed, gaping up at him. Raider flinched. Charlie hadn't been exaggerating when he'd said Van de Witt had gone to seed. The man looked bad. Really bad. There was little left of either the debonair banker or the rock-hard bandit leader. Van de Witt had lost a lot of weight, he was rail-thin, emaciated. His eyes were dark holes bleeding not light but loss. He had obviously shaved off his beard after leaving San Francisco, but his face was now covered by several days' stubble. His hands were shaking, but Raider didn't think it was from fear.

Van de Witt made an obvious effort to control himself. "So . . . now it's over," he said in his strangely hoarse voice.

"Yep."

"Well . . ."

"Well what?"

"Well, what are you waiting for? Why don't you shoot?"

Raider hesitated. Yes, why not? Hadn't he come here to kill Van de Witt? Like he'd killed Duval and Jackson? Because of what they'd done to Sarah?

But this was so different. Duval and Jackson had each been dangerous men, in full control of their faculties. Killing them had been an even contest. But to shoot this wreck, this ruin sitting on the bed in front of him, patiently waiting for a bullet . . .

"Uh-uh," Raider finally said. "I'm takin' you on in. You'll hang."

Now real alarm showed on Van de Witt's face. "Oh no! You can't do that. My . . . my family . . . my wife and children. Well, my wife is in an institution now, but my children . . . they'd hear about it. They'd know. They'd know that their father was hanged like a common criminal. They might even be forced to watch. People do terrible things to children. They . . . *You have to shoot me!*"

This last statement came out as a scream. Raider recoiled a little, then got himself back under control. "I don't hardly think it'd look too good if I just walked into your room and blew a hole in you, Van de Witt. Uh-uh. I'm gonna take you on in and see you hang."

"No! You can't! My God! I know you must *want* to kill me. You remember what I did to the girl . . ."

And now Van de Witt launched into an obscene description of Sarah's last few hours of life. It was all Raider could do to keep from pulling the trigger, but he refused to let Van de Witt goad him into killing him. It would be better this way, best to take at least one of them in and let the law have him. Van de Witt needed to hang.

Van de Witt must have read Raider's decision by looking at his face. He moved fast, then, taking Raider completely by surprise. He'd already gotten used to a man begging to be killed, but now there was a maniac coming at him with amazing speed. Raider tried to move aside, still not wanting to shoot, and then he saw Van de Witt's right hand swinging at his head, and there was something in it, something he'd picked up, and the next moment stars exploded inside Raider's skull and he knew he was falling.

He concentrated on staying conscious, of not blacking out, because he was sure Van de Witt would kill him if he did. He felt Van de Witt tugging at his .44, but he willed himself to hold on to it. A curse from Van de Witt, and then the man was no longer in front of him.

Raider realized that he had sunk down onto his knees. He could still not see clearly, there was a zone of blackness right in front of his eyes, shot through with red. But it was clearing now, and he forced himself up onto his feet. His head was throbbing. He touched the place where it hurt. There was some blood, but not too much. He wondered what Van de Witt had hit him with.

Raider could see clearly now. The room door was closed, and Van de Witt was nowhere in sight. Raider moved to the door and tried to open it. The knob turned easily enough, but the door wouldn't budge. It was designed to open outward, and apparently Van de Witt had jammed something under the knob.

Raider heard shouting outside, from the direction of the street, then a few seconds later the thunder of hooves. He began to kick at the door. After several kicks it started to splinter, then opened abruptly. A man with an angry face was standing in the hallway, one hand on the chair he'd pulled away from beneath the doorknob. "What the hell is going on in there?" he demanded.

His face whitened a little when he saw the gun in Raider's hand. "I'm after a man," Raider snapped. "The one who was staying in this room."

The man swallowed, still eyeing the Remington. "You missed him, then. He just stole a horse from out in front and rode off."

Raider ran outside. A small knot of men were standing together, looking toward the north, shaking their fists angrily. Raider's mount was on the far side of the plaza. He ran over to it and vaulted into the saddle. The men saw him. "He headed up toward the Trinidad road," one of them shouted after him.

Raider kicked his horse into a fast canter, following the man's pointing finger. There was no sign of Van de Witt, but Raider doubted that there were very many roads or trails leading out of here. The forests themselves were far too dense to ride through. If Van de Witt remained on horseback, he would have few choices of direction.

Raider kept his horse moving at a fast canter. If the chase proved to be lengthy, he didn't want his mount dropping out from under him. He remembered how Van de Witt, on his raids, had insisted that his men watch out for the condition of their horses.

However, that no longer seemed to be the case. About five miles up the trail, Raider met some men walking along the roadside. He stopped to question them. "Yep. A man came ridin' along here hell for leather just a few minutes ago," one told him. "Had his nag lathered up real bad."

Raider pushed on. Riding the way he was, obviously panicked, Van de Witt would pull away for a while, but when his horse began to wear out, it would be Raider's turn to gain ground.

Half an hour later Raider reached the small hamlet of Trinidad. It was situated above a deeply arched bay, the town itself consisting of only a few houses and a lighthouse. Here the land was a little more open; maybe the winds off the ocean discouraged trees. Raider could see all the way down the coast, to the big smoke cloud hanging over Eureka. Millions of acres of forest stretched inland. The air was clearer here, the sun bright.

Questioning the locals, Raider discovered that Van de Witt had ridden through only a few minutes ahead of him. When he explained that he was after a horse thief, the locals were happy to cooperate. "You'll git him, mister," a man told him. "The trail he took kinda dead-ends a ways up. And he was ridin' a real clapped-out animal. I don't think it'll last more'n a few miles more."

It didn't. Raider found Van de Witt's stolen mount about a mile farther up the trail. It was down on its knees, breathing heavily. Raider suspected that it would probably die.

As the man in Trinidad had told him, the trail more or less dead-ended here, becoming very narrow. Raider could see Van de Witt's boot tracks disappearing up a narrow track leading off to the left. There was barely room for a horse. Raider pushed his mount onto the track. He hadn't noticed a gun on Van de Witt, but that didn't necessarily mean he didn't have one. Raider rode carefully, watching for ambushes, but the cover here, while spiky enough to hinder riding, or even traveling on foot off the trail, was too thin to really hide a man.

The track ended another couple of hundred yards farther along. Raider rode out onto a broad meadow bordered by brush and small conifers. The sea lay about a hundred yards straight ahead. Now he saw Van de Witt, still running, but staggering badly from exhaustion. He looked back, saw Raider, tried to run faster, but there was really nowhere to go. In this open area, Raider would be able to ride him down easily.

Raider nudged his horse into a trot. Van de Witt veered to the side. Raider kicked his horse into a faster trot, to cut him off. The meadow was really a small plateau up above the ocean. The high bluffs at the seaward edge of the meadow were clearly far too steep to climb down. Van de Witt was trapped. Raider kept riding from side to side, forcing him toward the cliffs. He soon had Van de Witt pinned against the edge of a precipice, with a drop of at least a hundred feet behind him.

Van de Witt had no choice but to stop running. He stood on the edge of the cliff, facing Raider, panting, his face wild. "It's all over, Van de Witt," Raider shouted.

Van de Witt looked back over his shoulder, at the sheer drop behind him. Then he turned to face Raider. He suddenly seemed much calmer. "Yes," he said, his voice hard to hear over the sound of the surf, which was crashing into jagged rocks far below him. "It's all over. All over now."

When he looked back down the cliff again, Raider

knew what he intended to do. "No!" he shouted, urging his horse a little closer. The movement caused Van de Witt to take another step backward. "Tell my wife," he shouted. "Tell my children . . . No . . . don't tell them anything. Just let them believe I disappeared."

Raider jerked his rope loose from the thong that attached it to his saddle. He was still forming a loop when Van de Witt jumped. He simply stepped into space. In the instant before he disappeared over the edge, Raider was once again aware of how calm his face was. Maybe that was the way his wife, his children had known him, calm affection rather than the crisp efficiency of the banker, or the cold hardness of the boss. Just a man, a husband, a father.

Raider's horse had no intention of moving any closer to the cliff. He dismounted in one motion, racing toward the edge, then pulled himself back. The wind and rain had undercut the edge, and he found himself standing half in space. He backed off, then hunkered down, studying the shoreline below. It was all rock and wave, a maelstrom of land meeting sea. Then he spotted Van de Witt, a small patch of color on the bleak rocks, blood spreading around his broken body, quickly washed away by the water, and then a huge wave thundered inshore, wiping everything out in a cloud of spray and white water, and when the wave had gone out again, there was no sign of Van de Witt.

Raider stood at the edge of the cliff for several minutes, studying the surging water below. Once he thought he saw Van de Witt's body bobbing in the water about fifty yards offshore, but he couldn't be sure.

Finally, he turned and walked away from the cliff. He stood next to his horse, trying to figure out just how he felt. Cheated? No . . . just, well, kind of empty inside. They were all dead now, the men who had killed Sarah. And as each had died, his ties to Sarah had died too, one by one. Vengeance was a cold and tasteless dish.

Raider swung up into the saddle, looked back toward

the cliff again, then started riding slowly in the direction of the trail.

None of it had brought Sarah back. He was on his own again. Well, he'd been alone before. Maybe that was the way his life was meant to be—being alone. Something he'd been made for. That and his work.

# J.D. HARDIN

## "THE MOST EXCITING WESTERN WRITER SINCE LOUIS L'AMOUR"
### —JAKE LOGAN

| | | |
|---|---|---|
| _0-425-07700-4 | CARNIVAL OF DEATH #33 | $2.50 |
| _0-425-08013-7 | THE WYOMING SPECIAL #35 | $2.50 |
| _0-425-07257-6 | SAN JUAN SHOOTOUT #37 | $2.50 |
| _0-425-07259-2 | THE PECOS DOLLARS #38 | $2.50 |
| _0-425-07114-6 | THE VENGEANCE VALLEY #39 | $2.75 |
| _0-425-07386-6 | COLORADO SILVER QUEEN #44 | $2.50 |
| _0-425-07790-X | THE BUFFALO SOLDIER #45 | $2.50 |
| _0-425-07785-3 | THE GREAT JEWEL ROBBERY #46 | $2.50 |
| _0-425-07789-6 | THE COCHISE COUNTY WAR #47 | $2.50 |
| _0-425-07974-0 | THE COLORADO STING #50 | $2.50 |
| _0-425-08088-9 | THE CATTLETOWN WAR #52 | $2.50 |
| _0-425-08669-0 | THE TINCUP RAILROAD WAR #55 | $2.50 |
| _0-425-07969-4 | CARSON CITY COLT #56 | $2.50 |
| _0-425-08743-3 | THE LONGEST MANHUNT #59 | $2.50 |
| _0-425-08774-3 | THE NORTHLAND MARAUDERS #60 | $2.50 |
| _0-425-08792-1 | BLOOD IN THE BIG HATCHETS #61 | $2.50 |
| _0-425-09089-2 | THE GENTLEMAN BRAWLER #62 | $2.50 |
| _0-425-09112-0 | MURDER ON THE RAILS #63 | $2.50 |
| _0-425-09300-X | IRON TRAIL TO DEATH #64 | $2.50 |
| _0-425-09213-5 | THE FORT WORTH CATTLE MYSTERY #65 | $2.50 |
| _0-425-09343-3 | THE ALAMO TREASURE #66 | $2.50 |
| _0-425-09396-4 | BREWER'S WAR #67 | $2.50 |
| _0-425-09480-4 | THE SWINDLER'S TRAIL #68 | $2.50 |
| _0-425-09568-1 | THE BLACK HILLS SHOWDOWN #69 | $2.50 |
| _0-425-09648-3 | SAVAGE REVENGE #70 | $2.50 |
| _0-425-09713-7 | TRAIN RIDE TO HELL #71 | $2.50 |
| _0-425-09784-6 | THUNDER MOUNTAIN MASSACRE #72 | $2.50 |
| _0-425-09895-8 | HELL ON THE POWDER RIVER #73 | $2.75 |

---

**Please send the titles I've checked above. Mail orders to:**

**BERKLEY PUBLISHING GROUP**
390 Murray Hill Pkwy., Dept. B
East Rutherford, NJ 07073

NAME_____

ADDRESS_____

CITY_____

STATE_____ ZIP_____

Please allow 6 weeks for delivery.
Prices are subject to change without notice.

**POSTAGE & HANDLING:**
$1.00 for one book, $.25 for each additional. Do not exceed $3.50.

BOOK TOTAL      $_____

SHIPPING & HANDLING    $_____

APPLICABLE SALES TAX    $_____
(CA, NJ, NY, PA)

TOTAL AMOUNT DUE     $_____
PAYABLE IN US FUNDS.
(No cash orders accepted.)

# JAKE LOGAN